JOHN ROBB

◆

THE BIG HEIST

Complete and Unabridged

LINFORD
Leicester

First published in Great Britain

First Linford Edition
published 2011

British Library CIP Data

Robb, John.
    The big heist.- -(Linford mystery library)
    1. Gangsters- -Fiction. 2. Robbery- -Fiction.
    3. Robbery investigation- -Fiction.
    4. Suspense fiction. 5. Large type books.
    I. Title II. Series
    823.9'14–dc22

    ISBN 978–1–4448–0745–5

Published by
F. A. Thorpe (Publishing)
Anstey, Leicestershire
Set by Words & Graphics Ltd.
Anstey, Leicestershire
Printed and bound in Great Britain by
T. J. International Ltd., Padstow, Cornwall

THE BIG HEIST

Duke and his gang pull off the big heist, believing it to be the perfect crime. Stealing seven hundred thousand dollars from an armoured truck — the monthly payroll of oilfield workers — the gang get clean away with the fortune in treasury notes. But Duke overlooks one thing: the bills are in denominations of fifty dollars and upwards. The serial numbers, known to the police, will be quickly traced should the mobsters try to use any of the money . . .

Books by John Robb
in the Linford Mystery Library:

JAILBREAK
NO GOLD FOR TINA
FOUR CORPSES IN A MILLION
THE LAST DESERTER

1

Fifteen hundred miles of hard sweat. First through the Californian plains. Then over the mountain tracks. After that the desert. That is the drag from San Francisco to Chester City. It takes all of three days for the boys in the trucking business. Three days in which you curse and wish you were some place else.

Right now, Joe was cursing — at the sand mostly. He was still in the desert region, and the hard gritty stuff blew into his truck cabin. Then it worked into his mouth, into his hair, under his shirt . . . It made you feel like you were being rubbed over with a file.

But there was one consolation. The worst was just about over. Already in places the desert was giving way to patches of scrub vegetation. A few more hours and he'd be out of it. And by this time tomorrow he'd be in Chester City. Meantime, *Florrie's Pull In* was right ahead. It sure was a nice place to see.

Joe always stopped at *Florrie's* on this drag. It was the only place for miles around. A nice kind of place, too. There were always other truckers there, so a guy could have a talk. Today there were plenty of other trucks in the parking space in front of the wood building. A flash saloon, too, Joe noticed. That made it look like some tourists were slumming.

After the heat of the afternoon sun it was cool inside. But at first he could not see so well. Blinds were down on the windows and the eyes needed time to adjust themselves. But he saw Florrie all right. She was behind the counter washing cups.

Florrie said: 'Hiyer, Joe. Where've yer been this last month? You know I just can't get along without you.'

Joe grinned. 'I know that,' he told her, 'but I took a chance on you making out. I've been transporting down east. Only just been switched back to this route. I sure will be glad to see Chester City and crawl into my own bed again.'

She pushed a big cup of black coffee at

him. Joe sipped it and decided Florrie was okay. He was always deciding that when he and Florrie met. There was something comforting about Florrie. Fat and not so young. Sort of permanent. All the boys liked her. She even gave them credit when they were flat.

Joe could see things better now, and he looked around. A couple of truckers were sitting at one of the tables. They were reading newspapers. Three more were asleep, stretched on the benches that ran the length of the walls.

Then he noticed the folks who owned the swell saloon. They were at a table in the far corner. Joe was kind of disappointed. They didn't look like legitimate tourists. Not the sort who'd talk a lot of baloney, laugh out loud at rusty wisecracks, then maybe stake a guy a meal. You met that sort sometimes. But these seemed to be in a different category. You'd expect to meet their type in the city streets. In the narrow streets.

Three guys and a girl. They were huddled round that table and smoking like their lives depended on a regular intake of nicotine. The girl was only a kid. A good-looking kid. Long blonde hair to her shoulders and plenty of cosmetic slapped on her pan. But still only a kid. You could figure that by the shape of her legs.

One of the guys was high and fat. Another high and slim. The third — he was so small he looked like he'd been dehydrated. Joe thought it was their clothes that gave them away. Their clothes plus the way they wore them. All colour and no taste. A whole lot of padding, too, on the guys. It was funny, but just for a second Joe had a hunch those guys were watching him. Not watching him directly, but in a furtive kind of way. Under half-lowered eyelids. Florrie put a plate of ham and eggs in front of him. She said: 'I'll fill you up, Joe, before I forget.' Joe pushed over his vacuum flask. She filled it with boiling coffee. That coffee would help keep him awake during the long drive through the night.

As he was eating Joe thought: 'This joint ain't the same as usual. It's too quiet. What's happened around here?'

It was while he was scrubbing round the plate with a hunk of bread that he suddenly knew. It was the strangers. Those three slicker guys and the girl. They cast a sort of atmosphere over the place. Made it so you didn't want to say much because you didn't want them to hear. Even Florrie seemed to feel the atmosphere. She was still washing china. But she was doing it in silence. That wasn't like Florrie. Florrie was the kind of woman who'd have died in agony if she ever lost her voice.

Joe said to her: 'Your joint's getting like an art gallery.'

She moved up to him so she could answer in a soft way. 'I know it, and I'd be mighty glad to get rid of four of my oil paintings. They've been here most of the afternoon, and they don't add up to the kinda custom I like.' She finished with a hard glance at the corner table then went back to the china. Joe moved over to one of the long benches. He laid himself down and went to sleep.

It was getting dark when he awoke. Florrie had lit the oil lamps. Joe stood up and looked around. Two of the truckers had gone. Four new ones were in their place. But those three guys and the girl — they were still there.

But he didn't think much about them. He didn't think much about anything. His head was still clouded with sleep and he had to be hitting the road. He paid Florrie and eased out to his truck.

He made the routine check before getting in the cab. It was okay. The bar across the rear double door was locked good and firm. But you had to be careful when you were transporting a valuable load of silk. Particularly with these hijack boys around. Not that he'd ever met up with them. Never even so much as smelled them. Meeting up with them was the sort of thing that happened — but not to guys who were careful. Not to guys like Joe.

When the motor was running smooth Joe let in the clutch and bumped back on to the highway. Deep night had fallen when a saloon swept past him. It was

6

travelling fast, and its tail light soon disappeared. Joe didn't take much notice of it, except to think it was the only bit of traffic he was likely to see until daylight. After dark, the 'Frisco-Chester highway wasn't used much. But he was wrong. It was around midnight when he saw a car in the path of his beam lights. A saloon. It was drawn up against the side of the road. A girl had the bonnet cover up, and she was leaning over the motor.

Joe hesitated. *Speed Haul Inc.* put down firm orders to drivers. They were not to stop for anyone except the cops when they had a load behind. But not many drivers took a lot of notice of that. You just used your discretion. He was using his discretion right now. It was easy to see the pitch. This girl was having mechanical trouble.

Girls never could do anything about that. He felt kind of sympathetic as he switched his right foot from the gas pedal to the brake. He stopped a few feet behind the car. The girl straightened up as he got out of the cab.

Joe said: 'Maybe I can help you, sister.

What seems to be the trouble?'

The lights from the truck were full on her. She gave him a half-smile. Then she adjusted the coloured silk square that covered her head. 'I dunno. Motor just gave up.'

Joe eased towards the saloon. He was betting himself that she'd forgotten to put gas in the tank. That was the way girls were usually caught. He was about to handle the carburettor when he glanced at her again. That glance didn't do him any good. He felt a sort of quivering deep in his belly. The girl's hair was tucked under that square. But a few strands had broken free. They had fallen to her shoulder. Like that girl with the three guys in *Florrie's*. It *was* the girl who'd been in *Florrie's*.

And the saloon — it was the same saloon. He recognised it now. A new glossy Packard. But where were the guys? They didn't seem to be around. Joe thought: 'Hell! I'm getting' outta this — this could be anything!'

He turned to get back to his truck. But he didn't reach the truck. He didn't even finish the first step in that direction. Something seemed to explode against the back of his skull. It was like his head had suddenly been lifted away from his body and was flying off on its own. In the moment before he blacked out Joe saw the three guys. They were moving on his truck. With the bales of silk inside . . .

2

Captain Hollis looked heavily at a file. He looked at it as though he didn't like it, which was about the way he felt. It was labelled 'State Highways', and it was too thick for his comfort. He jabbed it with his thumb and said: 'It ain't getting better. It's getting worse.'

From the other side of the desk Dayle wondered when the old man was going to get to the point. He was new to the Larceny Bureau and when he'd first been summoned in here he figured he was due for some trouble. Now it didn't seem like it was exactly trouble. But it wasn't much better. Not listening to the chief bellyaching about hijackers. It was getting monotonous.

Hollis cleared his throat, and Dayle thought maybe he was going to say something worthwhile. Hollis was.

'Last night a trucker by name of Joe Mercer was slugged just inside our county territory,' he rasped. 'He's been seen in hospital, and he's in bad shape. But he recognised the mob as being with him that afternoon in a pull-in. Three punks and some girl. They worked the breakdown pitch, and Joe fell. He oughtta have known better.'

'Sympathy,' Dayle suggested, grinning. 'Those truck guys just can't resist a dame in distress.'

'Then that sure is a pity, because right now he's the one who's in distress. But quit the smart comments, will you? You ain't interrupting a college lecturer now. That truck was loaded with silk, and there's been a helluva lot of silk lifted the same way. It must be pulling a price, and it won't be so hard for the hoods to find just what trucks are carrying saleable stuff and what ain't. Anyway, they don't often slip up.'

Hollis got to his feet and lit his pipe. He continued when it was burning smooth: 'You've been groaning about not having much to do since you came into this department. Well, from now on that's gonna be changed. You'll be so busy you'll sleep with your pants on — if you sleep. I've a hunch that if we break up just one of those hijack mobs the rest'll scare off. That's gonna be your assignment. You can handle it any way you want. You can buy yourself a Sherlock Holmes hat and carry a magnifying glass if it'll help any. But get this — you gotta break the hijack punks in this area.'

Dayle fished a cigarette out of his jacket. 'Yeah — what have I got to go on?'

Hollis sucked hard at his dental plate. It was one of his ways of showing he felt sore. But only one way. He had plenty of others. 'There ain't a thing to go on. Hell, if there was do you think I'd be worrying any? I wouldn't. If we had just one lead all those punks would be in a penitentiary right now. But we haven't. The hoods hold all the best cards. The highways are lonely, and they are well organised. Take this last job they did. They musta had another truck of their own right on the spot when they slugged the driver. Joe Mercer's truck wasn't moved — only emptied.'

Dayle asked: 'Could Joe recognise any

of that mob if we showed him their pictures?'

'Only the girl. He didn't get such a good view of the others. That girl's just a kid, he says. Blonde with plenty of crowning glory. He's seen the whole picture gallery, but she ain't there. Musta just started in the racket.'

Dayle uncoiled his long length from the chair. He was still grinning. He was the kind of guy who finds life amusing. One of the minority. 'You're a shrewd cop,' he said. 'You couldn't have done better than give this assignment to me.'

Hollis was grinning too. He said: 'Didn't you learn about modesty when you were at school?'

'Sure,' Dayle told him. 'But I always was a dumb student.'

★　★　★

Palovi shrugged his thin shoulders. The gesture was intended to express regret. 'I sure am sorry for you boys, but I just don't want the stuff. Everyone's snatching silk bales now, and I've got more than I can handle.'

Duke ran fingers through his greased hair. He felt like working on Palovi. Like giving him the full treatment so he couldn't stand up for a couple of weeks. That's what he felt like doing. But he couldn't. When you need what another guy's got, you have to step light — especially when its dough you need.

'Come clean,' Duke urged. 'A month ago you'd have paid up five grand for that load and you'd have been singing as you counted out each buck. The bales are okay, ain't they? What's eatin' you?'

Palovi gave out a small and brief laugh. That laugh made Duke bunch his fists. But they were pushed deep into his pockets so Palovi could not see.

'Sure, they're okay. It's a nice consignment. But it takes time for me to unload stuff like that, and until then I gotta keep it some place. The more I have in stock the bigger the risk, and I have a whole lot too much in stock right now. Sell it some place else.'

Spoff decided to play a hand. Spoff was always deciding to play a hand. But he never seemed to play them right. He'd been sitting on a crate because there were only two chairs in the office. The Exalto Garage didn't have a big administrative department. It didn't do much real garage work either.

Spoff stood up and strutted towards Palovi. 'Listen, you shark,' he said. 'We can't sell the stuff any place else. You're the only guy we know who'll handle our stuff — '

It didn't go down so good except with Palovi. Palovi stretched his thin kisser into a smile. The others just looked at Spoff. And Spoff suddenly felt just a little guy.

Little and not so smart. Which was a pity, because Spoff spent a lot of time dreaming that he was slick and tough, like Duke and Al.

He didn't dare look at Duke. But somehow he felt him. Felt his iced fury. He wished he wasn't so scared of him — And it was the same with Al. He knew that Al was dragging on a cigarette as he watched him. Spoff wished he had Al's build. Real tall and plenty of what it takes. Al could bend a dime-piece between his hands. And he'd quit the

Army, too. Just quit because he didn't like it. And the Army were still looking for him. They'd go on looking. They wouldn't catch up with a guy like Al!

It was only Lucy that Spoff dared to look at. Lucy with the long blonde hair. Deep inside of him, Spoff knew a kindred soul. Lucy liked to think she was tough, too. But she wasn't, and that put her in the same category as Spoff. Anyway, Lucy was only a kid. He could meet Lucy's eyes. Spoff was wishing he'd kept his kisser shut. There was a nasty edge to Duke's voice as he spoke to Palovi.

'Spoff ain't so used to business methods. He's got the pitch wrong. We can sell this stuff some place else and get a nice price. But that'd take time and we don't want it on our hands that long. That's why we'll take three grand for it from you right now.'

Palovi laughed again. But it was still a caricature of a laugh. No humour in it. More like a death rattle. 'You boys've gotten me wrong. I ain't a charity organisation. But seeing you're so nice about wanting to do business with me I'll

16

pay out four centuries.'

Duke's breathing could be heard. It was coming deep and fast. 'Four hundred bucks! On the straight market that silk'd bring in all of ten grand!'

'That's all I'll pay and I'm not worrying if you don't accept. I don't want the stuff. It's a headache to me, like I told you.'

Under a thundering surge of emotion, Duke was trying to think clear. He thought of the work they'd put in on the snatch. The organisation needed to pick up that truck. The nice timing so they slugged the driver at just the right place on the highway. The risk of bringing it into Chester City to their garage. The expense of running this phony public garage so as to offer up a good and convincing front for the operations. And he was offered four hundred bucks! It would hardly cover the expenses!

They were being given the runaround. Palovi had started by paying nice dough and now he was skinning them. But they'd have to accept. He wouldn't offer a dime more. Not now that Spoff had opened up. If it wasn't that Spoff could handle a truck smart, he'd never be in the organisation. He was a dumb little runt.

'Okay,' Duke said, 'you've done yourself a smart deal.'

Palovi counted out the bills. All in fives and tens. And all old. Palovi didn't carry new money.

'I'll have the stuff picked up in an hour,' he said before he left the office.

And as they watched him walk through the garage and into the street, Spoff said: 'I'd like to fix that punk.'

3

Duke gave a hundred dollars to Al. Lucy got ten. The rest he folded and thrust into his pants. Spoff watched him in a surprised kind of way. Then Spoff asked: 'What about my cut?'

'You don't get a cut,' Duke told him. 'That's on account of you talk too much. Right now, you're a liability, not an asset. The rest of the dough's got to be kept with me if we're gonna stay in business.'

Spoff wanted to close up with Duke. Give him the one-two under the jaw, maybe. Then jerk the money out of his pants and split the thick end for himself. And have them all too scared to do a thing about it. That's what Spoff wanted to do. But you don't do things like that when you're only sixty-one inches high and turn the scale at less than a hundred and twelve pounds. Not unless you've got guts, you don't.

So Spoff bleated: 'Aw, heck, I've only

19

got a nickel! I need to eat, don't I? Give me somethin' won't yer?'

Duke threw a coin on the floor at Spoff's feet.

'There's another nickel. You're lucky. Now I've doubled your capital.'

Spoff picked up the coin and crossed to look out of the window. He wanted to go on thinking about the way he'd handle Duke if only he'd got what it takes.

Lucy said: 'We ain't gonna be able to do any more business with Palovi.'

She was buffing her fingernails and looking kind of thoughtful.

'You've got it wrong,' Al told her. 'We've just gotta hook the kinda merchandise he wants. He'll pay then.'

'Yeah. The first time, maybe. Just so's to make sure we come again. Then watch the market drop — same as it did today.'

Duke, who was sitting behind the desk, had the evening newspaper spread out in front of him. But he wasn't reading it. He was thinking hard.

Lucy gave him a quick glance. She was always giving Duke quick glances. Like she was afraid he'd get away from her sometime. 'What's on yer mind?' she asked. 'It won't do no good to keep on thinking about Pavoli.'

Duke ran a hand over his fleshy chin. After a pause he said slowly: 'I'm thinking about moving in on the real dough. The genuine stuff. Doin' it the direct way.'

There was something about the tone of his voice that made Lucy stop her manicure and Al pause in the act of giving himself a cigarette.

'You talk nice language,' Al said.

'Sure I do. And maybe we could fix ourselves pretty for a long time if we play the pitch right.'

Al said: 'Give! Are yer working out a fur snatch? Those trucks with furs in them ain't so — '

'Forget it. Forget furs, silks and all the other merchandise — except one — '

'You got me interested. We're listening.'

Duke indicated the newspaper. He'd circled a short news story with a pencil. 'There's an interesting piece here about the boys on the oilfields. It seems they're due for their yearly vacation when they collect their month's pay on Wednesday.'

Al lighted the cigarette. 'So what? The oilfields are always closed for a couple of weeks every year.'

'There are all of three thousand guys working there. Their payroll must add up to a helluva lot of sweet sugar.'

They looked at him in utter silence. Then Lucy said:

'The strain's tellin', Duke. An outfit like ours can't get in among that kinda currency. It's taken out there in an armoured truck and the guards don't carry peashooters, either.'

'We don't have to carry peashooters, either.'

Al worked up a grin. 'I'm thinking the same way as Lucy. You're goin' wild, Duke. It'd need a squad of the National Guard to shoot it out with those boys.'

'Who said anything about shootin' it out? The trouble with you is you don't have imagination. You don't think original.'

Lucy said: 'Okay, cut out the overtures and let's have the real music.'

Duke picked his words carefully. 'The dough's picked up from the bank by the

22

Mid-West Bullion Carriers. It's around a hundred miles to the oilfield and one of their armoured trucks takes it there on the Wednesday morning.'

'You ain't tellin' us anything fresh,' Lucy said. 'Everyone in the city's seen the truck setting off at the end of the month!'

Duke nodded. He'd hardly heard Lucy. He was feeling tense as he thought of the size and the prospect of his plan. 'Maybe one of you punks has heard about the big snatch from an armoured truck in the main streets of New York in 1932. That was really something. But I guess you don't go in for history.'

'I wasn't around in 1932,' Lucy told him. 'I've still got my own natural teeth.'

Duke added: 'That snatch was done by using tear gas bombs. The guards didn't have a chance. If I remember right, that was a cool million-dollar haul.'

Lucy was interested. 'You mean they got clear with all that currency?'

'Nope. They got over the hard part then balled it up by driving the truck into a tree — but we needn't do that — we could be smart — all we want is nerve.'

23

Al said: 'We'd need a helluva lot of nerve — and luck too. No, sir — I ain't interested. That ain't the same sorta proposition as sluggin' up a lone truck driver. Even if we did it, every cop in the States'd be on our tail.'

Duke pulled open a drawer, extracted a bottle of rye and took a pull from it. That calmed him.

He wiped his lips on the back of his hand and said: 'Have you thought about the sorta dough that truck'll be carrying on Wednesday? It won't be chicken-feed, There'll be enough to take us any place we want. We'd be on velvet. Don't that interest you, bud? I sure feel sorry for you if it don't, because there's nothin' more for us in the old racket. We're washed up, and you might as well know it.'

'Yeah — suppose we snatch the truck, we still ain't got the dough. The guards don't carry the keys, they're at the oilfield office.'

Duke was grinning. There wasn't so much force in Al's protests now. He figured Al was weakening.

'That can be blown open. And I know a

24

nice quiet place where we can do it. A place where we can get rid of the truck and organise ourselves before we move off. You can leave the fix'n' to me. I ain't failed yet, have I? All you have to do is to set up some of them tear gas bombs and get hold of four good respirators.'

Al had weakened. 'There wouldn't be any trouble about the respirators. There's a whole lot of old war stock still around. But the gas — it's not so hard to make; but a chemist'd have to do it. I think I know the guy. He'd want a hundred bucks — '

Duke said: 'This is the sorta talk I like. Keep that kinda attitude, and we'll be okay. Can't miss. Now come here all of you, and I'll give the whole pitch — '

4

The boys at the oilfield got a big kick out of the last Wednesday of each month. That was the day their month's pay arrived. The day they saw something back for the weeks of hard sweat.

But the rubbernecks at Chester City got something out of the day, too. They liked to stand around outside the bank and watch pop-eyed while the boxes of dough were lifted into the armoured truck. While that operation was on there were always a big bag of cops around. So many cops that it was sometimes hard to see over their shoulders. But those cops kind of added to the tension. The sort of tension an ordinary guy always feels when he's close up to a lot of dollars.

When at last the truck was loaded and locked and the guards were inside, there were so many folks standing around to see it move off it almost looked like a bridal car. This Wednesday was no exception.

The saloon was parked on the other side of the street and from inside it the mob watched the loading operations. They didn't talk much. They were feeling taut. Scared. But they didn't want to admit they were scared — not even to themselves. Spoff was in the worst condition. He sat behind the wheel and kept playing with the gears to relieve his nerves.

Sitting beside him, Duke thought: 'The yellow's comin' out. But it won't make any difference to the way he handles the car. I gotta hand one thing to Spoff. He sure can drive.

Al was with Lucy in the back. Once Al said: 'Pity we can't go for that sugar before it's locked in the truck.'

He was looking kind of hungry as the boxes were being stowed away.

'Sure. And it's a pity the oil firm don't make us a present of it so we don't have to go to any trouble at all,' Duke rasped. 'Right now, we'd never get near the dough. Too many cops around and too many rubbernecks as well.'

A few minutes later Spoff croaked:

27

'Have we got the highway diversion sign okay? We don't wanna forget that.'

'Relax,' Duke told him. 'It's right here — and this is where you start bein' busy. Get goin' — '

The last of the boxes had been loaded. The guards were climbing in the truck. The cops were starting to break the crowd up. There was a sudden relaxing of tension inside the saloon. The waiting was over. Now they were starting to do things. Spoff pulled across the stream of traffic and headed the Packard on the west highway out of the city. When they were nearing the suburbs they were halted by traffic control lights. Lucy was looking out of the back window. She said: 'The truck's comin' up. It's gonna stop right behind us.'

Duke cursed. He did it carefully and comprehensively. 'You gotta move fast,' he told Spoff. 'We need to get a clear ten minutes ahead of those mugs. I wish we hadn't had to hang around, but there was no way out. We had to be sure they moved off on schedule.'

Spoff was feeling a whole lot better

now he was driving. This was work he understood. Work he could do as well as any man. Right now, he was an important guy. 'You don't have to bellyache. That thing don't go so fast. I'll leave it clear behind. We'll have all the time we want.'

And that was how he fixed it. When outside the city limits he pressed hard on the gas pedal. That Packard could move, and it had plenty of encouragement from Spoff. Most of the time the speed needle was flickering around the eighties.

They'd been going for nearly an hour when Duke said: 'This is where you slack off. The secondary highway is on the right.'

They were moving up a long hill. At the top there was a side road. This made a three-mile loop, rejoining the main highway further along. It had been a connection with a quarry working, but it wasn't used now. Spoff turned the saloon up this road. He braked it among some trees at the side.

Duke said: 'We're doin' okay. We can relax for a few minutes I guess.' He gave himself a cigarette and tried to look easy.

Al was fingering his gun. Running his hand over the magazine and the trigger guard. It made him feel good. But it hadn't always been that way. He started remembering . . .

In the Solomon Islands — a foxhole — the Japanese were close. Maybe they were behind him. You never knew with the Japanese — he'd felt a sickness in his belly and a wildness in his head. Like he was delirious. The guy who shared the hole with him said: 'You don't have to worry about being scared, Al. We all feel that way.' But that guy had stayed where he was — Al had cut and run — got himself good and deep into the jungle and tried to stay there — figured maybe the Japanese'd take him and treat him good if he gave information. But the Japanese hadn't taken him. One of his own patrols had done that — walked right into them. He reckoned he'd been lucky to escape the death penalty. He'd been sentenced to life in jail — but they couldn't do that sort of thing. Not to Al. He escaped a few minutes after landing under escort in New York. Never seen the inside of a real penitentiary — never would either. Not him. Not Al!

Lucy said: 'This ain't any time to go to sleep, Al. You've got a tough assignment ahead.' He stopped fingering the gun. Stopped thinking about the past. He said: 'I can handle anything that's comin', babe.'

Duke glanced at his strap watch. 'We've been here ten minutes,' he said. 'Let's get goin'.'

Al got out of the saloon. Lucy passed him a varnished wooden sign. A sign that had been lifted from the Highways Department.

'See you time it right,' Duke told him. 'We don't want any private cars turning up here.'

Al said he wasn't to worry. Then he walked down to the main road. He looked down the hill. There wasn't a lot of traffic around. An open roadster went past with a woman at the wheel. Then a farmer's jeep heading in the direction of Chester City. That was all. All until the armoured truck came in view.

He saw it when it was a mile off at the bottom of the slope. It looked just a speck.

Like a toy out of a kid's shop: But he could hear the grate of gears as the driver changed down. There was no other vehicle about.

Al moved on to the centre of the highway and put up the sign. It read ROAD DIVERSION. Under the words there was an arrow. The arrow pointed up the secondary road.

Then Al placed himself among the trees and waited. 'We're all set,' he told himself. 'This is gonna be interesting. This'll sure make the headlines.'

There was just one chance of a slipup. That could be if a private auto overtook the truck and followed the diversion sign. There would be no time to get it out of the way, then put it back. The result could be awkward. But it was the sort of chance you just had to take.

They were lucky. Except for the truck, the road stayed clear. From his station among the foliage, Al watched it draw close. It slowed to a walking speed when it came in sight of the sign. He could see the driver leaning forward to read it. He started talking with the three others who were in the big cab. The sun reflected the silver of their uniform buttons as they twisted and gestured.

The truck stopped. It stopped within twelve feet of where Al was standing. He could hear their voices now. And he didn't like it any. Didn't like being so close. Didn't like what they were saying. 'Yeah, but we weren't told of any diversion when we set out,' the driver said. 'I figure we shoulda been told. We're supposed to be wised up of there's anything outa the ordinary about the roads. I guess we'd better just go right on. The highway repair boys will let us through!'

Someone else answered: 'That's a dumb idea. Suppose they don't? Then we gotta come back and start again. No, sir — I wanta be home before midnight. I'm plenty familiar with this scenery without volunteering for an extra dose of it.'

The driver wasn't convinced. 'I reckon they'd let us through. We gotta priority.'

'We'll need more than a priority to get us over a road that ain't there — and that could be. This loop road ain't so long to travel. Let's go.'

33

A third voice said: 'Sure, let's go. If we stand around here much longer it'll be time to bring the oil guys their next month's pay.'

The driver seemed to hesitate. But he decided he was overruled. The armoured car turned into the secondary road. As it did so, Al pulled away the diversion sign.

He threw it into a ditch. Then, still keeping among the trees, he followed the truck.

Duke's end had done okay. They had parked the saloon dead across the highway with no space to get past at either end. The truck had braked in front of the obstacle when Al rejoined them among the trees. He rejoined them all except Lucy. Lucy was in the car. She was slumped over the steering wheel, like she was in a faint.

The boys put on their respirators and picked up a supply of tear gas bombs while they waited. Those bombs felt comfortable in the hand. They'd been made by pouring the liquid gas into electric light bulbs. The ends had been sealed over with rubber.

One of the guards got out of the cab. He walked cautiously towards Lucy. He had his gun out. Those boys were getting kind of suspicious. Which was natural.

Duke had expected this. The rest was up to Lucy. She had to make them feel it was okay, so they'd all get out of the cab.

The guard opened the saloon door. 'What goes on, sister?' he asked in an uncertain way.

Lucy stayed slumped over the wheel. Her long hair fell among the spokes. She gave out a whimpering groan.

The cop looked around. Then he put his gun back in its holster and pulled Lucy against the back of the seat.

Her eyes flickered. Then they came open. There was a look of dazed wonder in them. She was doing a swell act.

'I'm asking you what happened, sister?'

She shook her head, like she was trying to clear it.

Then she spoke. It was a faint, apologetic quaver. 'Gee, I'm sorry. I guess I didn't see that diversion sign until the last second, and I took the turn too fast. Got into a skid and hit my head on the wheel.'

The guard's face cleared. It became sympathetic. He turned to the boys in the truck.

'The dame near piled herself up because of the diversion. She don't look so good. Maybe we oughta take her along with us until we find a cop. She could be a hospital case. You gotta be careful with concussion.'

Lucy groaned. A nice, ladylike groan.

'Yeah — I don't feel so good. It's — it's my head — '

The other guards got out of the cab. They crowded round the saloon. The driver said: 'I'd better shift this Packard outa the way.'

They started to lift Lucy out of the seat. Three of them did that. All except the truck driver. He was looking down at the road.

They were carrying Lucy clear when he said: 'Does this dame claim to have skidded?'

'Sure thing. That's how she slammed her head.'

The driver became tense. He felt for his gun.

'There ain't no marks on this road, so it's been a mighty gentle skid. I don't like this. I smell a phoney. Let's get back to the truck fast.'

It was then that the boys went to work. They did it systematically. First Duke sent over a couple of bombs that fell in front of the cab doors. At the same time Al and Spoff pitched theirs into the cluster of guards. The effect was better than they'd expected. Because there was no breeze, the irritant white vapour rose in dense clouds, and the guards almost disappeared among them. For the first few seconds the boys worked while still concealed among the trees. Then they moved forward, respirators on.

The guards got their guns out. But they could not use them. You need to see to shoot. And their eyes were closed, swollen, streaming with water. They were choking too, as the stuff rawed their lungs. They tried to get back to the truck. One of them did just that. He stumbled out of the main cloud of vapour, and as he reached the cab he was in another. But the others stumbled around like they were blindfolded.

37

Inside the close-fitting rubber of his respirator Al started to laugh. As he crashed the butt of his gun against the skull of the nearest guard he thought: 'Geeze! — it's too easy.'

That was the way it looked. Knocking those guards cold was like trapping tame rabbits.

They got them among the trees. They stripped off their uniforms before knotting and gagging them. Then the boys pulled the uniforms over their own clothes.

They didn't look so good on Duke and Spoff. Particularly Spoff. But Al was okay. He'd have passed for a guard in any place. As they moved back to the road Spoff asked: 'How long will it be before these bums are found?'

Duke glanced back at the sprawled and still unconscious figures.

'I dunno. Maybe not this century. I ain't worrying.'

Then they saw Lucy. She was reeling about the road rubbing her eyes. The clouds had dispersed now, and she could see a little. But only a little. Lucy looked like she was a professional mourner.

'You slobs forgot about me,' she breathed. 'One of you could've pulled me outa that stuff.'

Duke grinned. 'Aw, quit squawking. You knew it was gonna be tough. Now get into the saloon and start driving. You know where to go. We'll be seeing you at the farm.'

Spoff got behind the wheel of the truck and backed it on to the main highway. Lucy followed with the Packard.

5

It wasn't such a long drive to the farm. Duke figured that was where he was being clever. The cops'd expect them to move off a long way fast. But they weren't doing that. Just a matter of forty miles maybe. That was all. But it was an ideal hideout. It couldn't be bettered. Duke thought he'd been smart there too. It was only by chance that he knew about it. Once a guy on the run had hidden up there. That was a long time ago, but he'd told Duke, and Duke had remembered.

It was a disused farmhouse. It had been disused for years. Soil erosion from the desert had made it impossible to scrape a living out of the place. Which meant it was nice and lonely.

As the truck bumped up the narrow track towards the farm Duke gave himself a big hand. He told himself he was something more than a big shot. He was the sort of guy all America would be talking about. The guy who organised a payroll snatch and took a whole armoured car. That was a laugh. Particularly when you thought about the guards lying about in their underpants. He wondered what Palovi would say if he knew how much currency they had under their control right now.

Duke leaned back in the cab. He felt almost luxurious. Yeah, that was the word. Luxurious. It was luxury that was coming to him. Food, drinks, dames —

The farm building consisted of a single floor shack. Most of the windows were missing, but it was built from heavy timber and in good repair. There were a few outbuildings, but they were rotting. The place looked bleak as they came in sight of it.

Spoff braked the truck in what had been a barn. Lucy was right behind in the saloon. When they were standing together in the barn Al said: 'I guess the first thing's gonna be to check on how much dough we got.'

Duke nodded. 'Yeah. Then we gotta get rid of the truck. That'll be easy. There's a deep river near here. It'll go in there. But we'll pull out the dough first.'

Al opened up the boot of the saloon. He brought out a small wooden box. Inside the box were four sticks of a yellow-brown substance. Gelignite.

Instinctively they stood back while Al very gently broke a piece off one of the sticks. This he inserted under the steel bar that secured the truck door. Then he went back to the boot and produced a length of cotton fuse tape. He tucked an end of this behind the gelignite.

'Okay,' he said. 'Scram!' And he lighted the fuse.

They drew well back from the barn, taking cover behind an angle of the farmhouse building. The explosion was almost disappointing. Nothing dramatic. Not so loud as a .280 rifle. It was like the bursting of a paper bag. That was all. But the results of the explosion were impressive. For a few seconds tiny fragments of steel were whirring through the air. One piece buried itself into the wall on the shack.

They eased back to the barn. That

gelignite had done a nice job of work. The door bar looked like it had been chewed away. And it was hanging limply open. One of the hinges had been smashed.

Lucy and Spoff made a run towards the truck. They were over-anxious. They came to a dead stop when they saw inside.

Lucy said: 'Hell — we still can't get at the dough.'

She was looking at a second steel door that fitted flush in the back of the truck.

'Not yet,' Al told her. 'Not for quite a time, babe. I gotta be careful how I blow this one open. We don't want to damage that currency. You go into the shack and fix some food. We'll be needin' it when we're through.'

Lucy looked undecided. Like she didn't want to be parted from the locality of the dough. Duke said: 'You heard — get goin'.'

She pulled some tins of food from the back of the saloon and went to the shack. As she pushed open the unlocked door she thought: 'Geeze! This dump looks like it's part of the dust bowl.' It wasn't such a

43

bad description. There were only two rooms. The floors of each was laden heavy with dust and sand. The walls were of bare logs. And the only furnishing was a table and a few crude chairs.

Lucy made herself busy with a tin opener. Outside she heard an occasional small explosion. Not much more in volume than a cough. That was Al working through the second steel door.

The last explosion had taken place when Lucy came out of the shack. She'd opened up the tins and left them on the dusty table. There were no plates to empty them on. Then she'd sat herself on one of those dusty chairs and thought. Thought about the time she was gonna have with the dough. The swell clothes. Not second best, like she was wearing. The best, and plenty of them. Maybe Duke had been cooling off a bit lately. But he'd stop cooling when he got a load of her in the outfits she was gonna buy. She'd have all that it takes then! She walked up to the truck.

'Gee,' she said as Al and Duke lifted away the safe door, 'you've got it open.

Now we can have the count.'

'Beat it,' Al told her. 'We're busy.'

Lucy watched them for a moment as they sweated under the weight. But Duke gave her a mean look. So she went over to the saloon and switched on the car radio. A dance strain was coming through. A trumpet was being handled strong and pure. Lucy started to shuffle her feet. Then she danced, her heels tapping on the hard, sandy ground. She always wanted to dance when she heard music. But especially today. Today she felt good. The music faded. The announcer started to read the news flashes. Lucy turned up the volume. She wanted to listen to this. So did the boys. They paused in their work on the truck so as to hear better.

'I guess we'll be featured big,' Lucy called over to them.

Duke told her to close her pan.

Then it came. The announcer said the guys in the oilfields were having to wait for their pay following the snatch of the armoured truck that morning. He gave the details. It seemed one of the guards had managed to crawl to the main

45

highway and give the alarm. There was the usual bellyaching about all roads being watched. Currency to the value of seven hundred thousand dollars was involved. They grinned at each other. Seven hundred grand. That sure was serious dough.

The announcer added: 'All the bills are in denominations of fifty dollars and upwards. The serial numbers are known and have been circulated as part of a nationwide police emergency action. The money will be quickly traced back to the mobsters if they try to use it.'

Lucy spoke first. But it was a long time before she did speak. Then her tones were hollow. 'That's a bluff! They're tryin' to put the scare on us. They haven't got the numbers of the bills!'

Duke, leaning against the side of the truck, was looking right through Lucy, in a thoughtful kind of way. He said: 'We'll soon know. We gotta get them boxes into the shack.'

There was a bit of a shake about his voice. It sounded dry and brittle. They carried the bullion boxes inside and piled them on the table. Several trips were needed before they were all assembled.

Duke gesture to Al. 'Open them up!'

That wasn't difficult work. The lids were only clipped down and sealed. They didn't worry themselves any about breaking the seals. As each box was opened, Duke lifted out the bills. All were in neat blocks, held together by a paper band. All were new. They were consecutively numbered. Most were for fifty dollars each. A few blocks were for a hundred bucks. One held only two-hundred buck bills. They made a deep heap on that table. Most were still in their paper bands. But some were breaking loose.

Al said urgently: 'Well — let's have it. Are they okay? They sure look good.'

Duke gave himself a seat. He lighted a cigarette. His hand wasn't steady. And his fleshy face looked like bad yellow cheese. He didn't answer. They all watched him. Like wolves watching meat. Lucy was fiddling around with her bag. Fastening and unfastening the clasp. But she was not aware of what she was doing.

'What is this?' she asked, her voice a bit shrill. 'Have you given up talking? Struck dumb or something? Give us the strength. Is that dough good?'

Suddenly Duke looked old. Looked like he would normally appear in another twenty years. His lips were grey now, and there were lines from the corners of his mouth up to his nostrils. 'The guy on the radio wasn't kidding,' he mouthed. They waited for him to say some more. But he didn't. He just sat. Heavy and aged.

Spoff watched him curiously. He'd never seen the boss like this before. The boss looked weak. He seemed like he'd become the sort of guy that Spoff could handle. Spoff decided to take a chance. He eased up to Duke.

'Start talkin',' he rasped. 'We want to know all the pitch!'

Duke raised his face. He gazed into Spoff. And from that moment Spoff decided not to talk any more. There was death — pure unadulterated death in those eyes.

Slowly Duke stood up. He put a hand on Spoff's narrow shoulder. Spoff shrank away, but not far; Duke was holding him as he growled: 'Listen, chicken bit, you give me that line just once more. Go on — just once more. I'm listenin'. I want to hear it again — '

Spoff felt a big lump develop in his throat. Two dabs of sweat appeared on each side of his forehead. 'I didn't mean nothin',' he croaked.

Duke twisted him round, so Spoff lost balance and fell to the floor. He stayed there. He figured it was a whole lot safer.

Duke pulled on his cigarette so that it showed a quarter inch of glowing red. He was looking at the logs of the opposite wall as he said: 'If we spend just one of those bills the cops'll have us. They'll trace it back inside twenty-four hours. I know. They have their system, and it can't miss.'

Lucy looked desperately at the pile of currency. 'You mean we ain't got any dough at all! Not even a few bucks?'

'I mean just that. This dough's hot. We can't touch it. I just didn't figure on it being made up in high value bills. I guess they make up the small amounts from cash held in the oilfields office — those boys are smarter than I thought. They're a whole lot smarter than I thought — '

6

Captain Hollis said: 'The bank have just listed the serial numbers on those bills. I've had them flashed to the radio stations and the newspapers. Inside an hour, everyone who handles money'll be looking out for them.'

Through the window the lights of the city flashed amid the darkness. They reminded Dayle that he was tired. Tired of trying to get a lead on this hijacking assignment.

Hollis seemed to know how he felt.

'When you're new to this department you expect things to happen fast,' he said. 'Mostly they don't. I ain't blaming you for not getting anything yet on the hijack boys. I knew when I gave you the job it'd be hard going. But I'm thinking maybe you could start paying some attention to this armoured car haul. It was hijacking, but on a really big scale.'

Dayle laughed. 'I'll say it was. The boys

who planned that musta been crazy or desperate.'

Hollis pressed tobacco into his pipe and nodded. 'Usually when they do that kinda work they are desperate. Maybe the bottom was falling outa the easier racket.' He was fingering a blue slip of paper. 'I have a report here. It's just a routine affair. But it could tie up, so I'm passing it on to you. This report says there's been no one at the Exalto Garage for a couple of days. It seems some customers leave their cars there, and they are wanting to get them out. They're feeling kinda sore about it.'

Dayle said he'd feel sore in their place. Then he added: 'What gives you the idea this could be a lead?'

Hollis held up a hand in caution. 'I haven't got that idea. It's just playing off a hunch, and it could easy be wrong. But get this. That garage has been run by Duke Bellas. We haven't got a thing on him, but he's never smelled exactly sweet. Now it seems he's disappeared as well as his garage being locked. It's worth a check-up.'

Dayle nodded. But not with much enthusiasm. He didn't feel a lot of hope. A whole lot of hunches had fallen down lately. As he stood up he asked, 'When are you breaking in that garage?'

'Right now. A patrol car's waiting to leave. You'd better join it.'

Dayle eased out of the captain's room and to the elevator that took him down to the ground floor of the department. His eyes kept closing. He wondered when he'd see his bed.

He guessed he'd never been so tired since the war. Since those days when he was on the Solomon Islands — when you couldn't sleep because if you slept you died. Maybe he'd been more weary then than now. Right now he was in clean clothes. He had eaten. He wasn't screwing up his nerve watching and waiting for Japanese.

But some guys hadn't endured the strain. There was that bum who ran into his patrol. Quitted his foxhole. A big, tough looker. But he couldn't have been so tough. Must have had a long streak of yellow — he'd shot at them, at his own men, so as to try to get free. He was a rat. But he'd heard he'd got away when he was landed at New York. Maybe it was a pity he hadn't been up against a firing squad.

One of the cops in the patrol car said, 'You sure look fatigued. Maybe you'd like us to push you along in a wheelchair.' Dayle worked up a grin as the car speeded along the streets, which were almost deserted. It was after two o'clock.

The double doors of the Exalto Garage were barred. But that didn't delay the boys any. They wrenched the padlock.

It was a musty sort of place set in a side street. A lot of oil on the concrete floor and a few autos parked around. He left the patrolmen and eased into the office. Dayle decided it was the kind of office where nobody did much work. Papers were littered about like confetti, There was dust on an old and battered typewriter.

A moth started to circle round the unshaded light bulb,

At first Dayle thought: 'These boys ain't been able to pay their creditors. It seems like they've gone into voluntary liquidation.' But he didn't think that a few minutes later. Not when he glanced at the evening newspaper that was spread on the desk. Not when he saw the news story, which was circled in pencil. A news story that told about the oilfield workers going on vacation after collecting their month's pay.

Dayle folded the newspaper and pushed it into his pocket. He said to himself: 'It looks like we're going places.' And he no longer felt tired.

7

The morning sun came in through the broken windows of the farm shack. Lucy was grateful for its warmth. It loosened her limbs after a cold night of sleeping rough on the floor with only a rug from the car as a covering. But that was all she was grateful for. There was simmering fury in her eyes as she tried to smooth the dirty creases out of her costume. Her stockings were laddered. That long hair of hers needed attention. A lot of attention. She glared at the boys.

They were sitting round the table, and they didn't look so smooth either. Beards were sprouting out of their pans. They were haggard. Worn. Like guys who were beaten. Lucy walked unevenly towards them. It was an uneven walk because one of her shoe heels had been wrenched off by the rough stony ground outside. She said: 'Just how much longer are we gonna stick around here? We've been in this dump for three days, haven't we? In that time we've eaten outa tins, and we ain't had enough to make a canary flourish. I ain't stickin' it any longer.'

Duke didn't bother to look at her as he answered: 'You'll stick it as long as I say, sister. Pipe down.'

'Yeah! Then what are we gonna live on? The food's done. We only brought enough for one night. We gotta get some food. Then we gotta get outa here.'

Al fidgeted in his chair. He could only think of cigarettes. It seemed days since he'd had a cigarette. He'd give most anything for a smoke. 'The dame talks sense,' he told Duke. 'We gotta move sometime. We gotta — just gotta.'

Duke rubbed a hand round his bristled chin. He knew he must look awful if he looked anything like the rest. 'We ain't movin' outa here for another couple of days. It ain't safe. The area'll be stiff with cops. We gotta wait for things to cool off.'

Lucy's voice reached a shrill pitch. She had her hands on her hips. 'Another couple of days! What are we gonna live on? Tell me that, smartie! I don't need to go on any slimmin' diet, and I ain't aimin' to.'

Duke said: 'It won't hurt you any. Blondes mostly run to fat anyway. Maybe this'll hold it back some!'

She glanced towards a corner. The boxes were piled there. The boxes with the dough sticking out of them. The sight hypnotised her. This was currency. Not just some currency. Hundreds of thousands of dollars of the sugar. It was what they'd worked for. And right now they were living like a mob of hoboes. All that dough there. And she hadn't even a clean dress. And she was hungry. Real hungry. She'd never been like this before.

It was an effort to pull her eyes away from those boxes. Her tones were more even when she said: 'Listen, why don't we split that dough and make a break for it. We could get over the border maybe. It's a chance. We could cover thousands of miles before the first bill was traced.'

Al said: 'Sure we could. We could travel fast with that currency. Maybe they'd never catch us.'

Duke breathed hard. 'Listen, you

punks. Sure you could travel a long way. Maybe you'd get over the border. But what good'd that do you? Every bill you spent'd be a new clue. Even if you got into South America you'd be extradited.'

Lucy's slim body seemed to ripple with fury. 'That's what you think. Maybe that'd happen to you. But I'm smart. They wouldn't catch up with me. I know my way around.'

Duke pushed back the chair and stood up. He looked at Lucy first. Then Al. Then Spoff. He bunched his fist and brought it down on the table. He bellowed:

'Listen! Because I ain't tellin' you again! That dough's hot. It's so hot I don't like even to touch it. But we've got just one chance. That's to lie low and not move outa here for another two days. Then maybe we can use some of the currency to move fast over the border. Then do you know what we're gonna do? I'll tell you. We're gonna burn every bill that's left. That way there's just a chance we won't be traced, because we can't spend what we don't have. But right now the whole area'll be crackling. We just have to hold on here a while. It ain't safe to put our heads outa this shack.'

Al and Spoff seemed impressed. It was the first time Duke had given them a line on getting clear of the place. But his reasoning didn't carry any grist with Lucy. She gave out her thoughts in a series of semi-shrieks.

'You mean we're gonna burn the dough! *Burn it!* Boy, I'd rather do a life sentence than that.'

'You will — if you don't,' Duke assured her.

She said just two words low under her breath. Then she looked again towards the boxes.

★   ★   ★

Late afternoon. It was like an oven in the shack. That was the worst of the place. It cooked you during the day and froze you at night. You could get used to the dirt. But not the changing temperature.

The boys were sleeping. They were not sleeping because they were tired. It was

60

because there was nothing else to do. Duke was across two chairs. His hands were folded across his big belly. A fly crawled uninterrupted over his crinkled hair.

Al and Spoff were on the floor. Every few minutes they turned so as to give relief from the hardness.

Lucy had her handbag open. She was gazing into the mirror that was fixed inside it. And with her free hand she was dabbing powder from a compact on her face. The powder didn't altogether hide the dust marks. But it helped. She brought out the stick of rouge and rubbed it over her lips. That made a big improvement. She glanced again at the boys.

Al turned and groaned. But he was still sleeping. None of them looked like waking. This was how they'd spent every afternoon in the shack. They'd become conscious again when the sun was down.

Lucy took off her shoes. They'd make too much noise. Particularly the one without a heel. In her stockinged feet she moved towards the boxes.

A kind of electric thrill went through

her hands and percolated into her body as she touched the bills. Thousands of bills. New and clean. With a nice sort of smell from them. She took a block of the fifty dollar denominations. She wasn't going to be wild. She was going to play this smart. Just take as much as she'd need. Lucy peeled off four of the bills. Two hundred bucks. That ought to be plenty for a dress, stockings, and a nice supply of food. But maybe she ought to be on the safe side. Might as well be sure. She took away another couple of bills. Three hundred. That was better. She could face up to anything now. Lucy pushed them into her handbag.

Then she eased to the door. It made some noise when she opened and closed it. But she got through okay. Outside, she put her shoes on and crossed to the barn.

The saloon was in there. But not the armoured truck. That truck had been driven into the river nearly forty-eight hours ago. Spoff had done that job.

If Lucy had started up the Packard's motor right then she might have awakened the boys. But she wasn't going to do

62

that. She had it all worked out.

The barn was at the top of a slight slope. The slope led down a track, and it joined the highway a mile off. Lucy settled herself behind the wheel. She freed the handbrake and let the car roll.

She was almost at the highway when she started the motor. The deep tones from its eight cylinders made her feel more confident. She had a car. She had currency, She was going places.

Lucy figured it would take her around thirty minutes to reach Parry Falls. She'd heard Duke mention that it was a score of miles from the farm. A small town, he had said, and a place where a lot of cops might be gathered. But Lucy wasn't scared. No sir, not Lucy. The cops'd be hunting for three guys and a woman. Not a woman on her ownsome.

The time estimate was right. Lucy came into the main street inside of half an hour. And she hadn't seen a cop or anyone else on the way. Duke was getting yellow. There wasn't a thing to worry about if you played the cards right. The shops looked okay for a one-horse town.

But right now any shops would look okay. It was good, real good, to see people around again.

She parked the Packard and started to walk along the sidewalk. But after a few steps she remembered her shoes. That was the first thing. She'd got to get herself some new shoes.

In the shop an assistant fitted her out with a couple of pairs. One in lizard skin. The other smooth blue leather. They were slim and slick. And they cost plenty, but they were worth it. She put on the lizard skins and the others were packed for her. The girl in the cash-box took her dough without even glancing at her.

Right next door there was a milliner's. Lucy spent quite a time looking in the window. There were two models that sort of got her. Both were bright coloured dresses. One, in blue silk, would go nice with that spare pair of shoes. The other, a white creation, had a kind of purity about it that pulled.

It was quite a big store. Anyway, bigger than you'd expect in this town. A tall woman with a lot of fuzzed red hair took her into a fitting cubicle. That woman was looking curiously at Lucy's soiled clothes.

'I had a flat in my auto,' Lucy told her. 'I had to change the wheel when I was coming in here.'

The strawberry blonde said sure, she understood. Nothing was worse for a gal than having to change a wheel.

Those two dresses were a good fit. They didn't leave a lot of change out of a hundred bucks. They seemed glad to take the dough. Maybe it wasn't often they did business so easy! It was the same at the beauty store where she laid in some cosmetics. No trouble. Just no trouble at all.

And so far she'd only seen one cop. That cop was on traffic control duty and looking like he was half asleep. Next she took the Packard further down the street and stopped it opposite a food store. 'I'm goin' camping,' Lucy told the old man behind the counter. 'I want stacks of canned stuff.' He was plenty courteous. He carried the load of provisions into the back of the saloon.

But when he saw the fifty-buck bill he

said: 'Ain't you got anything less, lady? That'll use a lot of my small change.' Lucy looked, but she couldn't make it up in small bills. He had to take the fifty. By now Lucy realised that she was hungry — and thirsty. The excitement had made her forget about eating for a while. But she might as well eat now. There was a smart-looking saloon over the road.

She found a table under one of the cooling fans. She ordered a five-dollar steak. It came to her smothered in onion sauce. It tasted okay, and so did the tall iced lager with it.

Lucy was going to tell the waiter she wanted her check when the youth with the pimples came up. He'd been leaning against the bar talking to a pair of other slobs. She'd noticed that he'd kept giving her the eye, but that didn't worry her any. She'd been too busy with the steak. Anyway, she was used to men looking at her like that. Now this punk came to her and stood at the other side of her table. He had a slack mouth that showed bad teeth. Sweat was glistening round his small eyes. And, of course, he had those pimples. Clusters of them.

He said: 'Hiyer. I don't like to see dames like you around on their own. You need company. I'd sure be glad to offer some.' Lucy gave him the freeze. She did it by looking at him and through him. And by saying just nothing.

But the punk with pimples wasn't discouraged. That sort of guy didn't have to be discouraged easy, otherwise he'd never get any place. He sat himself beside Lucy, pulling the chair close.

Lucy waved to the waiter. He brought over the check. And that waiter was grinning. Like he'd seen this kind of thing before and was enjoying the routine.

She paid him with dollar bills and rose to go. The punk took a hold on her wrist.

'There ain't no hurry, sister. I'm giving you an invitation. Try to be sociable.'

Lucy pulled, but his grip was tight. She couldn't get her arm free. By now a whole lot of the customers were watching. That waiter, too. But none looked like doing anything about it. Lucy suddenly figured that maybe this wasn't such a nice joint.

She breathed: 'Listen, hick, if you don't lay off, I'll fix you.'

He took that like it was a rich crack. He laughed and half turned to his buddies at the bar. He repeated her words to them. Then they all laughed. Lucy was getting scared. She figured she'd had enough. She wanted to be getting back to the shack. Her right foot whipped forward and the point of her new shoe slapped against his anklebone. Lucy knew where to kick. But still Pimples held her wrist. He groaned under the pain and stood on one foot, but he maintained the grip!

Lucy saw the tall glass out of which she'd been drinking the iced lager. She tried to break that glass over his head. But he caught her free arm, and now both hands were locked. Lucy twisted and writhed like a crazed snake. The table overturned, and in the confusion Lucy broke free. Pimples made another grab for her. His fingers closed on the new white dress. It tore down a side seam as she ran to the door.

Now the waiter got in her way. He was looking mean.

'You don' get away that way, sister,' he said. 'You've done a whole lotta damage here. We'll want compensation.'

She groped in her bag, gave him a fifty-dollar bill, then rushed towards the car.

* * *

Lucy was turning up the track towards the farm shack when she realised that her dress was torn. And she'd left the parcel with the spare one in the saloon. And the spare shoes. And the cosmetics. It was when she noticed that the lizard skin shoes she was wearing were dented in at the right toe that she broke.

She started to sob.

She'd never been really scared before. Not like this. It was as though her innards were embalmed in ice. It took her a long time before she was able to open the door of the shack.

The boys were waiting for her. Particularly Duke. She stood just in the threshold trying to control the sobs. Between those sobs she gave it all to

Duke. She let him know every detail.

When she had finished he said evenly; 'We're gonna have to get outa here today. But not until it's dark. That'll give me time to give you some hints on doin' as yer told, Lucy. Just a few nice quiet hints. But before I do that, you'd better put the Packard in the barn. We'll be needing it, and I don't want it left around so it can be seen.'

She stumbled out into the dusk. Her chest was heaving as she restarted the motor and headed the car for the derelict barn. It wasn't so much what Duke was going to do. It was those clothes. And those shoes. Right now, she was worse off than when she set off. Now she'd nothing to wear. Nothing at all. She'd left her old stuff at the stores.

Maybe it was her tears that prevented her seeing properly. Maybe it was just that she didn't care any more. That she'd exhausted all her emotions except that of disappointment. It could have been any of a lot of reasons. But she drove the Packard into the side of the barn. And she did it at quite a speed.

When she got out she was unhurt. But the front axle was bent back. The car was a grade-one wreck. The car in which they had been due to make their getaway.

8

Three fifty-dollar bills. They weren't exactly new now. They'd lost their first freshness. They were crumpled in places. But they still were far from being old. They hadn't yet been stained by the grease of scores of fingers. They lay on Captain Hollis's desk.

Hollis brooded over them as he said to Dayle: 'All paid into the bank at Parry Falls. That's all we know — so far. You're gonna see to the rest. I told you when I set you on this case it could be handled just any way you liked. But let me give you a tip. We know it's Duke's outfit we're after. They could still be in that locality. Don't go to that town telling everyone you're a plainclothes cop. Word might get around. Ever done any hunting? Yes. Then maybe you'll know a scared animal is the hardest to trap. Try not to scare them too soon.'

Dayle eased round to the garages at the

back of headquarters. There he fixed up for the loan of a car. Not a big car. Just an ordinary cream-coloured roadster like a travelling salesman might use. The mechanics there got busy with the back of that car. They fixed four steel rods just below the roof.

The rods were only just in place when a pile of women's frocks arrived from a wholesale warehouse. The police organisation was getting to work now. The frocks were suspended from the rod, and they made a vivid show.

The boys were grinning in the police garage when Dayle drove the roadster out. Dayle was grinning too. He felt a different guy now he was going some place. Getting some place.

It was around one o'clock when he drove into the main street of Parry Falls. He braked outside the bank. Inside, he told the teller: 'I wanta speak to the vice president about an account.'

He was shown into the room of a quiet spoken, elderly man. When he was seated Dayle said: 'You've had a call from headquarters at Chester City to say I was coming. After I've left here I want you to forget you've seen me.'

The vice-president nodded. He understood.

Dayle asked: 'Can you give the names of the customers who paid in the bills?'

The vice-president said he could in the case of one customer only.

'We don't usually note the numbers of bills being paid in,' he said. 'There isn't the time. They are checked later during the daily audit. But the teller remembers who paid in one of these bills. That's because it came from a small trader. Not the sort who generally handles fifty-dollar denominations. The teller remembers that this one was credited to the account of Mister Kam. He keeps a food store. I sure am sorry I can't help you about the others.'

Dayle told him the information was enough. He got back into the roadster and drove down the street until he saw Kam's food store and delicatessen. Kam was serving some women with provisions. Dayle stood back and watched him. It never took him long to assess a character.

He decided that Kam's character was okay.

There was something brisk and direct about him. He moved about in a clean and decisive sort of way. There was an American Legion badge in his coat. Dayle decided he could trust Mister Kam. Which saved a whole lot of trouble.

When the store was clear of customers Dayle said to him: 'I'd like to speak to you alone for a few minutes.'

He flipped open his identification ticket. Kam's eyes went wide when he saw it. 'Sure thing. Come right into the back.' He lifted the counter flap and Dayle was led into a small living room. He didn't like having to do it, but Dayle began by reminding him of the Civil Security Laws. Kam nodded.

'You don't have to worry. If I can help the law I will. If what you're gonna say to me is in confidence, then it'll stay that way.'

Dayle asked him about the fifty-buck bill. Kam was fast on to that. 'Sure — it was handed to me the day before yesterday by a blonde dame. She was going camping — she said. She took away

75

a whole lot of canned food. I remember her well because I asked if she could give me something smaller in the way of currency, but she couldn't.' Kam poured a measure of bourbon in a couple of glasses, passed one of them to Dayle. When they were drinking Dayle said:

'That bill was from the bullion truck raid.'

Kam damned nearly dropped his glass. He looked blank. 'Gee! You don't say! I just didn't think about that when the blonde was in here. I never thought any of that mob'd start spending the dough in my store. I figured they'd be a long way from this area.'

Dayle said: 'There's a good chance they're still around here. That's what I aim to find out. And I gotta find out fast because that mob's mighty dangerous. They could be killers. Do you know this country well?'

Kam said he did. Dayle asked him to find a map. A big-scale survey map was found and spread on the table.

'I want you to mark all the places these boys could be using as a hideout,' Dayle told him. 'Then maybe you'll loan me the map.'

Kam hesitated. 'I'll do my best, but that ain't so easy . . . Suppose we draw a fifty-mile circle around Parry Falls. Inside that circle there'd be a helluva lot of possible places. Most of them are derelict farms. A lot of farms around here have gone to bits because of the desert sand blowing in.'

'That'll be my worry. Just mark all the places you know. I'll get around to them.'

It took Kam quite a time to pencil the map. Several times he was disturbed by the demands of customers.

When they shook hands Kam said: 'It'll be just too bad for that mob if the boys from the oilfield get a hold on them. Those boys had their vacation delayed.'

Dayle left, deciding that he liked Kam. He eased along to the local police headquarters. It was a small one-floor brick building. The lieutenant in charge at Parry Falls was kind of excited when Dayle introduced himself.

He said: 'Say, what goes on? I'm itchin' to get my men out on a hunt for these hoodlums, but I ain't had any orders from Chester City. I can spare six men and they can run the comb through this area.'

Dayle gave him a slow grin. It was the sort of grin that folks just had to like.

'We want you to stay in reserve. If they're still around we've first got to locate them. That's best done the quiet way and it's my assignment. But just keep your men ready in case you get a call from me. If that call comes it's liable to be urgent.'

Reluctantly, the lieutenant grinned back. Back in the car, Dayle studied the marked map. As he drove out of Parry Falls the women's frocks swayed gently on the steel hanging rods.

* * *

Kam's markings hadn't been altogether accurate. That wasn't surprising. They weren't intended to do more than suggest possibilities. The first two farm shacks he visited had been reoccupied by optimistic folks who figured they could do something with the land.

78

At the first one a grizzled old-timer told him to clear off. He didn't want to buy no fancy clothes. At the second he found a customer. He knew people were living in the place as soon as he saw the scraggy hens around. But it was too late to turn back. He had to go through with being a salesman.

A woman emerged from the cabin. Dayle figured she was the biggest thing in skirts he'd ever seen. Her body swelled out in a huge circle like it had been inflated with compressed air. It was covered by a straining, greasy smock. She must have weighed all of two hundred pounds. Whatever other hardships she was suffering out here, it didn't look like starvation was one of them. She looked mighty pleased when she saw the clothes in the back of the roadster.

Dayle got out of the seat and gave her the sort of grin he figured travelling salesmen should give to prospective customers. She grinned back.

'Say, this sure is enterprise,' she told him. 'I could use a new dress. Lemme see what you've got.'

She wrenched open the door and pushed herself in among the materials. The side of the roadster creaked and lowered under her poundage.

Dayle said cautiously: 'I don't know that I've got just your fitting, ma'am. Maybe I'd better come again with some more samples.'

She was pulling the frocks off the rods. Her voice sounded a bit sore. 'You ain't leavin' here till I've gotten me a new dress. The old man ain't around and this sure is my chance. That bum wouldn't stake me for anything.'

She emerged with an armful of flowered frocks. She didn't say any more as she rolled back into the cabin.

Dayle thought he'd like to move off right now, but that wasn't the sort of thing a salesman would do. He gave himself a cigarette and waited. As he waited he watched the chickens. They looked like they didn't see much future in life. Dayle wondered whether the fat woman was giving them all their feed ration. They looked kind of cheated.

The silence was broken by a sound of

tearing material from inside the cabin.

The woman bawled out: 'You don't have to worry. That was my old smock!'

There was another period of quiet — or almost quiet. It was sometimes broken by faint muttering from the 'invisible' woman. Like she was working out a problem aloud. Then the window was pushed open a few inches. Three frocks fluttered to the ground. Her voice screamed: 'I'm keeping two and joining them into one. That way I guess they'll be a good fit.'

Dayle retrieved the rejected stock. From inside the voice said more softly: 'What's the cost, mister?'

He decided on a rock bottom quotation. 'Ten bucks for the pair.'

'The hens are five bucks each. Take a couple of brace of them.'

Without thinking about it, Dayle glanced indignantly into the cabin. He looked away again quickly. He said: 'I'll call again sometime when you have the dough.'

She sounded pleased at that. She said he was the sort of salesman she liked to meet. Her old man'd be pleased, too.

Dayle stood on his cigarette butt. He asked: 'Could there be any more customers around here? Any new folks maybe?'

There was a pause before her voice came through. 'There could be. A couple of days ago my old man said he saw a saloon climbin' up the track to Deed's Farm. He was a long way off, but he saw it clear enough. It was kind of funny, because that place's been empty for years. The land ain't no good at all. If anyone's bought it, they sure are gonna face hard times.'

Dayle gave himself another cigarette. 'Maybe they can still afford to buy. Are you sure it was only two days ago he saw the saloon?'

'Yeah. It was late in the afternoon. He's thinkin' of goin' across himself, sometime, to see if any folks have moved in.'

'How do I get there?'

A bare arm that would have been okay for a heavyweight fighter emerged from the window. It pointed to some distant hills.

'Right over there. You can't see the

track from here. It's too far off. But get down to the highway and follow it along. You'll find it then.'

Dayle didn't even wait to tip his hat before getting into the roadster.

9

Spoff came in from the barn. Sweat was rolling down his thin pan and mingling with bristles on his chin He looked desperately at Duke.

'It ain't no dice,' he said. 'I just can't get that axle fixed. It's got a bend on it like a spring. I'd need a steam hammer.'

Duke cursed. He sat on the edge of the table and twisted his fingers.

'You've taken one helluva time to find that out. Two days ago you said maybe it could be done. What's the matter with you? It's just this sorta work that you're on the outfit for.'

Spoff looked towards Al and Lucy. There was no sympathy from Al. Al was watching him like he wanted to tear him apart. Lucy huddled in a corner. She wasn't even listening. She hadn't been taking much notice of anything since Al had slapped her down.

'We'll have to make the break without

the saloon,' Spoff urged. 'We can do it. Maybe they won't think anything if we travel outa this territory on foot. Yeah — that's right — we could be on a hike! The cops'd never think twice about some boys on a hike!' His voice faded out.

Duke, who was gaping at him hard, said: 'There ain't never been such a dumb punk. Do we look like we're on a hike? I'll tell you what we look like. We look like what we are — an outfit on the run. And how long do you think it'd take us before we dare use transport? I'll tell you. It'd take us days. And all the time we'd have to spend dough to stay alive. We'd have to spend that hot dough. The chow Lucy brought up's about done. And we've been here too long already. The cops'll be visiting all these shacks. They'll be here sometime.'

Al walked towards the window. He said: 'They ain't gonna take me. I ain't staying here to be taken like a rabbit. No sir. I'm gonna make a break for it with some of that currency. I'm gonna buy me a bath and a shave. And a soft bed for the night. Then I'm gonna figure out the next move. Right now, in this stinkin' place, I can't think.'

Duke got down off the table. He eased up to Al. Silently, like a fat snake. He put a hand on Al's shoulder and twisted him around so they were face to face.

Al's voice was on velvet as he said: 'Don't do that, Duke. It don't pay to push me around.'

Duke dropped his hand. He didn't want to have to tangle with Al right now. If he had to handle Al, he'd do it in his own time, by his own methods. But he spoke tough. 'The nearest you'll get to a soft bed'll be in a cop cell,' he rasped. 'And in those places they don't go in for double-thick mattresses. I know we gotta move. We can't wait no more. I know that. But we're gonna move the smart way.'

Al relaxed a bit. Spoff, who had been nibbling at a tin of fish, stopped nibbling. Even Lucy looked up from her corner. Lucy looked in bad shape. There were bruises on her face.

Spoff said through the fragments of fish: 'So you've still got some ideas.'

'Sure I've still got ideas,' Duke replied. 'What do you think I've been doin' these past five days? Sittin' on my fanny and writing poetry? I've been figuring things out, and since that no-good broad busted the saloon, I've had to figure fast.'

He looked around to be sure they were all listening. Then he went on: 'We're gonna snatch a car. Spoff's gonna do it for us. He's gonna take one out of a parking space where there ain't much chance of it being missed right away. Then we'll start for the border. After a time we'll snatch another car, then maybe another. That'll make it harder for the cops. There's an even chance of getting over the border if we do it that way and do it right.'

Spoff didn't look like he was altogether satisfied. He pushed the fish-tin away. 'You say I'm the guy who's gotta do the first car snatch?'

'Sure. You're in charge of transport in this outfit.'

There was a trace of a whine in Spoff's voice. 'So I'm gonna run most of the risk, I have to go into Parry Falls. What if I'm picked up?'

Duke said: 'That'd be just too bad. But you won't be if you're smart.' He looked at his strap watch. 'It's near five o'clock. If you get down on the highway now you'll be able to thumb a ride into Parry Falls. Tell any yarn you like. When you've got a car you head right back and stop a couple of miles short of here. We'll be waiting for you.'

Spoff said he thought it'd be okay.

'It'd better be okay,' Al said, 'I'm sending you because you're the least likely lookin' guy among us to be snarled up in a bullion lift. But get this. If you try any double-cross, I'll get you. So help me, I will. I'll get you, Spoff, if I have to wait fifty years and chase you to Europe.'

Spoff shivered. He didn't like Al when he spoke like that. He was different somehow. Cold as death. He looked towards the boxes. 'Maybe I'd better take some of that dough.'

'You don't take any dough. Not a cent. You go like you are. If you took any of that currency you might get the idea of making the break on your own. I don't want to put temptation in your way,

Spoff. It wouldn't be fair.'

Al was looking out of the smashed window. Suddenly he licked his lips. They had gone hot and dry. He said: 'None of us are goin' any place for a while. There's a car coming up the track.'

Duke gave out a short curse. The breath left Spoff's lungs in a low moan. They looked out. They were all looking out — except Lucy. She was still on the floor. But now there was a faint smile on her pan. It might almost have been a smile of relief. Relief that soon it might all be over.

Duke's brain was working in high gear. He whipped round to Spoff and Lucy: 'You two get in the other room and keep quiet. Al and me'll handle this. That car has a lot of clothes hung in the back. He could be a salesman.'

Spoff was glad to be out of the way. He pulled Lucy to her feet and dragged her into the other room. Before the door closed behind them Lucy said: 'Did someone say that guy was bringing clothes? Gee, I'd like to meet him.'

Duke and Al watched the car stop.

They watched a tall and hunky guy get out and look around. He moved to the shack door.

In a hiss, Duke said: 'We're farmers. We've just taken over this joint — '

Al nodded. He also felt inside his jacket pocket until his fingers closed over his gun. He intended to keep his fingers there.

There was a rap on the door. A firm, confident rap.

Duke pulled back the bolt. As soon as Dayle saw the filthy and unshaven figure he thought: 'This is the guy. This is him. He fits the description,' but aloud he said; 'Howdy. I sure hope you don't mind me walking in on you. As a matter of fact, I didn't think I'd find a soul here. This farm's been empty for years, but I always pay a call when I'm around just in case folks have moved in. I sure am lucky this time.'

He was grinning. His pan looked cheerfully dumb. The door was still only half open when Duke said: 'Are you sellin'?'

'Sure. And I only sell the best, mister.

Clothes for the ladies. All Paris designs. Maybe you'd like to give your wife a treat, eh?'

'My partner and me are out here alone and we don't have wives. We're not in the market. We've got plenty to do with our dough getting' this land into shape.'

Duke was looking hard at the guy. He seemed okay. Anyway, it didn't matter much if he wasn't. He couldn't do anything by himself. And they'd be out of this dump when Spoff had snatched a car — when he snatched a car. Duke was looking again at the cream roadster. It was a nice vehicle. Small and not too flash. They could use this all the way to the border because, if they handled things right, no one would be looking for it. Maybe the arrival of this bum was a gift. Maybe it was the way out. Yeah — it *was* the way out.

Duke tried to look like he was changing his mind: like he was in the middle of a mental tussle. Then he said; 'Maybe we could do business. I have a gal and she might be comin' out here. A new outfit sure would go down well with her. Come right in.'

He held open the door, and Dayle eased into the shack. To his nostrils the place ponged like an old sink.

'You sure have a lot to do to make this place comfortable,' he told Duke, who agreed affably while he got a grip on his gun.

Al was standing in the corner beside the boxes. He'd just placed a length of sacking over that dough. When Dayle saw him he thought: 'That bum ain't new to me. I've come up against him before. It was a long time ago. I sure wish I could remember where . . . '

But he said to Al: 'Hiyer. Your partner thinks maybe we can do business with some dames' clothing. I sure have a nice selection. All exclusive models and at nice prices too. I sell clothes for the masses — that's me. You won't complain about my prices.'

Al didn't answer. He was wondering about this punk. Wondering where he'd seen him.

Duke asked: 'You often around this territory?'

'No, not so often. Twice a year maybe. Tonight I'm heading right back to Chicago. I gotta pick up new stocks from the warehouse there.'

Duke gave him a twisted sort of grin. He said that was fine.

Dayle suddenly became aware that both of them were watching him. Watching him intently. He wondered if they were satisfied. Maybe his act as a salesman wasn't so smart. Or it could be that they were scared to let anyone go who'd seen their hideout. But he'd thrown in the piece about making straight for Chicago to cover that. Still they were watching him. He decided he'd seen enough. He was going to get out and give a general alarm. From now on this was work for the uniformed boys. It might be tough getting them out of this shack.

They looked like they'd shoot.

'I figure I'd better bring in my stock so you can take a gander for yourselves,' he said briskly. 'You sure will like what you're gonna see.' He turned towards the door.

Duke was blocking his path with a gun.

That gun was steady and aimed at the centre of the belly.

'Don't worry any about those dresses,' Duke said quietly. 'We can look at them without your help.'

It was a bad moment. Dayle decided to go on being the salesman. He said: 'Say — are you boys thinking of lifting my stock? If so, it ain't worth your while It ain't worth all that much.'

As he spoke he eased a fraction closer to Duke. He figured he might be able to get hold of that gun. Might be able to twist it out of his hand. It had been done before from such a position. The move was taught in the police combat school.

Then he remembered Al. Or rather, he heard Al, Al was coming up behind him. Dayle turned to see what he was doing But he only got halfway round when something crashed on to the side of his skull knocking his hat over his face.

He was unconscious before he hit the floor.

★ ★ ★

Lucy had carried the dresses into the shack. She regarded them like they had done her some personal harm.

'They ain't any good,' she announced. 'They're just goddamned cheap muck. I've never been around in stuff like that.'

The boys didn't answer. Each was putting a thick block of dough into his pockets. Duke said: 'We don't need to take too much. We only spend when we have to. And the rest's gonna be burned when we reach the border, like I told you.'

Lucy looked up from the dresses. 'Say, you still talkin' about burnin' all that currency? I still say you're crazy. We could find plenty use for it if we're smart.'

Duke said: 'You don't wanta say goodbye to all that do you, Lucy?'

'I sure don't. I wanta stay right among it.'

Duke laughed. So did Al and Spoff. 'Then that's what you'll do, Lucy. You'll stay right among it,' Duke said.

For just a second she looked pleased. Then a scared expression spread over her bruised face. 'Whatd'yer mean, Duke?'

'I mean you're stayin' right here. From now on you ain't any asset. And you have too many bright notions of yer own. So we're leavin' you in this shack along with the salesman.'

Lucy's eyes went wide open. A muscle at the side of her lips started to work. 'Gee — you can't do that. I'm one of the outfit. You can't two-time me that way.'

'Can't we sister? Wait and see. What'yer bellyaching about, anyway? You said you didn't want to say goodbye to the dough. I'm fixin' it for you so you won't. You'll have all the currency you want while yer strapped up in here.'

She ran to him. She grabbed his coat. 'You're not goin' to do that. Not strap me up and leave me in this dump. I'll never be found. I'll die.'

Duke put a hand on to the middle of her face. He pushed her away. She collapsed on to a chair.

'If it weren't that I don't see no point in getting any more raps hung on to me, I'd give you a slug right now and fix you for good. But the chances are you'll be okay. The cops'll be arriving here inside of a few days. I guess that's a certainty. You might be alive when they find you.'

Spoff started to look anxious. He said: 'What if the cops arrive sooner than that? She'll tell them where we've gone, and the salesman'll give them the licence number of the car.'

Duke shook his head. 'You worry too much. It's getting dark now. They won't be checking on places like this in the night. And even if they come tomorrow, we can be just about at the border by then. The way you can drive, we'll be well into South America before they can organise anything.'

Al had an idea. He was looking down at the inert figure of Dayle. Dayle had been trussed with lengths of cord they'd taken from the windows. The boys had made a pretty good job of him. His wrists were joined at his back and they were strung to his ankles. He was still unconscious.

Al said: 'We may not have to use this hot dough; That guy oughta been carrying some money, and it'll be cool. We could use that.'

Duke was pleased with Al.

'You get smarter,' he told him. 'We've not checked his pockets yet. Frisk round them.'

Al bent down and opened Dayle's jacket. He gave out a low, short whistle. 'Have you ever known a travelling salesman carry artillery?' he asked.

Duke and Spoff leaned over, while Al held back Dayle's jacket. A leather holster was visible over his left shoulder. It contained a heavy revolver.

Duke pushed Al out of the way. He groped in Dayle's interior pocket and pulled out his wallet. It contained money and a social security card. That was all. Duke kept the money.

He had to search for quite a time before he found what he was looking for. It was in a small concealed pocket just under an armpit. And it was a cop's identity paper. This one was overstamped with the words

Larceny Bureau — Special Service

They all looked at the paper — all except Lucy.

Spoff made the first comment. It was an excited kind of whine. 'Say — we've just gotta finish him off. And the dame, too. We can't leave them here now. Not the cop, anyway. If we do, we might never get clear.'

But Duke had that tight smile on his pan. He was looking almost tolerantly at Spoff. Almost. 'Relax. Don't strain yourself,' he said. 'Right now the pitch just couldn't be better for us. That flatfoot's been doin' a tour of this territory to find us. His headquarters can't know he's here because he hasn't had a chance to tell them. So how does it add up? I'll tell you. It means there ain't a chance of the cops being set on our trail for days, because even when he's missed it'll take plenty of time to find him. By that time we'll be nicely on our way. This is just about perfect. We have a roadster outside, we have cool dough.'

Lucy started to yelp. She stretched forward in the chair. 'Say, you're not leavin' me alone with a cop? I won't have a chance if you do that. Maybe they'll give me fifteen years. Hell! Have a heart, Duke.'

'Shut yer kisser,' Duke told her. 'You're being sorta optimistic. With this new set-up I'm not sure the cops will come along in time to help you. They are certain to take quite a few days. In this climate you won't starve to death. But I guess you could get more thirsty than's comfortable.'

'You mean I could die of thirst! Hell! I won't let you do it, I tell you, I won't — '

She acted with surprising speed. As she broke off the sentence she sprang from the chair and flung herself towards the door. That door was still open. She was through it before the boys had collected their wits.

Then Duke bawled: 'What'yer waitin' for? Get her.'

Lucy slammed the door shut as she rushed out. It was almost dark. The moon wasn't yet up and there were a lot of deep shadows round the derelict farm building. She was level with the barn as Al and Spoff emerged from the shack.

Fifty yards from the barn there was a small wood of stunted redwood trees. This led down to the river. She did not hesitate. She ran for the wood.

Lucy had a high turn of speed. She was helped by hollow, gripping fear. A fear that drove her muscles beyond their ordinary capacity. Al was all of twenty yards from her when she plunged among the first trees, Spoff and Duke were still further behind. It was quite dark there in the wood. The branches and the leaves shut out all the light.

Invisible branches tore at her arms and face. Her bruised face. But she did not feel them. When she was well inside the wood she turned off at an angle. She plunged on for several minutes. Then she stopped. She stopped because she had to. Because her body couldn't take any more. She was panting like a whipped animal as she fell among the rotting leaves and the bushes.

As he got into the wood Al thought: 'If I keep still I'll hear her moving.' But he couldn't. Couldn't because of the row Spoff and Duke made as they tore into the undergrowth.

Then Duke started bawling: 'Come outa there Lucy. Don't be stupid, baby.

Maybe if you come out we can talk things over.'

Lucy heard his voice. It came to her faintly. But she did not take in the meaning. Her eyes were shut, and she was in a half faint.

After a while Duke called Al and Spoff together. They spread out and started to work down towards the river. When they reached the river they had not found Lucy. It seemed impossible to find anything in that dense darkness. They gathered in a huddle at the side of the water.

Al said: 'We gotta bring her in. We can't let her float around.'

Duke looked into the black mass of the trees. He was thoughtful. He said: 'We could hunt all night without finding her. What's the difference if we leave her? She's too scared to come out of there before morning. Then she'll still have to lie low because of the cops. She can't harm us any.'

10

It was cold in those woods. And kind of uncanny, too. Lucy felt a wave of hard trembling seize her body like she was being picked up and shaken. Faintly, she'd heard the boys move away in the direction of the shack. But the sound didn't mean much to her. It didn't have a lot of significance. Right now, she was in no sort of condition to work things out.

Even when she heard the faint throb of a car engine and the clash of hurriedly engaged gears it didn't give her any encouragement. It was a long time later that she suddenly realised that the boys were no longer around. The car had gone. They were in it.

She tried to think what to do. But she couldn't. Her flesh was paralysed. Her mind was the same way. Lucy gave out a brief, tortured whimper. She mumbled: 'Geeze — aw, Geeze — ' Then she slid off into a faint. This time it was a deep and complete faint. It was almost daylight when she flickered open her eyes. She was looking up at an iron sky that was already flecked with blue.

In the trees the songbirds were tuning up, and the sharp edge had gone out of the air. There was a hint of the coming heat of the day.

It took her quite a time before she could remember why she was there. And when she did, she started to sob again. But not for long. Her belly was too empty for her to go in for much of that kind of emotion. It felt like it was a hollow tunnel. And her throat was as dry as baked felt. But there was the river. She could do something about her throat with the river there.

It wasn't so easy to stand. The cold and the night dew had etched deep into her bones. Every joint was stiff, and they gave pain when she moved them. She advanced a few yards at a time, holding on to trees and bushes, as she reeled down the slope to the water.

At the riverbank she lay flat and drank with her face in the stuff, like some animal. Then she dabbed her features with the hem of her tattered dress. Lucy felt better now. Not much better, but still, better, and she was able to figure things out. Right now she was on her own. She had no dough and she was in bad shape. No woman could do much under those conditions. Help was needed. Any sort of help. Even the sort a cop would give.

She stumbled towards the shack. The door was half open and the first thin sunlight was streaming in as she entered. Dayle was within a few feet of that door. During the night he'd twisted and rolled towards it with a sort of vague idea that he'd have a better chance of freeing himself outside the shack.

Blood from his head wound had seeped through his hair and dried on his face. His skin had gone a chalky grey. From the floor he looked up at Lucy in a flat and puzzled way.

Lucy said softly: 'Hell, you sure are in bad shape — almost as bad as me, I guess.'

There was a long pause while Dayle absorbed the fact that this girl had come back. By some miracle she'd got away from the mob. Without thinking much about it, he'd figured that Duke would have converted her into cold meat before now.

Then he said: 'Get these cords off me, kid.'

She moved as though to start untying the knots.

'It'll take you most of the day that way,' he told her. 'My jacket's somewhere around. There oughta be a knife in it.'

She found the folding knife and sliced through the bonds.

At first Dayle's limbs were dead. Lucy bent down and started to rub his wrists and ankles. It was hell as the blood again started to flow, but inside five minutes he was able to stand and move around. He asked her what had happened after she'd quit the shack. Lucy told him. Dayle put on his jacket, found a cigarette and lighted it; while he listened.

When she'd done he said: 'You did the right thing in coming right back here, even if there was nothing much else you could do. You're all set to make things a lot easier for yourself, but you're not through yet. You can still be a whole lot of help to me if you want to. *Do* you want to?'

Some of the craft came back into Lucy's eyes. 'Say — would I get a State pardon?'

Dayle eased towards her. He put a hand on her shoulder.

'Right now I can fix it so you go in for fifteen years. Maybe twenty years if the judge ain't feeling so good. I can also give evidence that'll mean you won't waste all your youth and beauty in a penitentiary. But there won't be any pardon. You're in it too deep.'

It was in a near-whisper that Lucy said: 'Okay. I'll help all I can.'

They went down to the river and Lucy watched while Dayle took a turn at freshening himself up. When he'd done the dry blood was off him, but he still looked rough. Then they started to walk down the track to the highway.

There they sat on the grass verge and waited. There was never a lot of traffic here, and for the first half-hour nothing went past. Then a coupé appeared travelling fast towards Parry Falls. Dayle thumbed hard. The driver slacked speed slightly, then as he drew level he stepped on the gas again. Dayle muttered. 'I ain't blaming him. We don't look like the kinda people travellers would want to carry with them.'

The next time they had a better deal. An ice-cream refrigeration truck came along. This driver wasn't so particular. He stopped and leered at Dayle and Lucy.

'Been out for the night?' he asked, giving Lucy the benefit of a lot of attention.

'Yeah,' Dayle told him, 'and right now we're feeling kind of weary. We aim to get to Parry Falls.'

'That's a long walk, mister.'

Dayle moved nearer to the cab door. 'Not if you take us along.'

'Okay. But it'll cost you ten bucks.' Dayle decided he didn't like this bum. There was no charity about him.

'I don't have that with me, but you'll get paid when we get to Parry Falls. I got friends there.'

'I have, too, mister. But they don't hand me ten bucks for the asking. I want the dough now or you don't ride in my truck.'

Dayle decided he'd taken enough. He'd been pushed around a lot in the last twelve hours. He decided to do some of the pushing himself. It'd make a change.

He pulled open the door and jumped into the truck. The driver slapped his hand on the gear lever, but he didn't get any further than that. There wasn't any point in going any further. Dayle had switched off the motor and pulled out the ignition key.

Then he said: 'I've changed my mind about paying you ten bucks. Maybe the dough wouldn't do you any good. You look like the sort of guy who'd only waste it. You're taking us on this trip for nothing, and you're doing it because you're made that way. Because you're big and generous. That's the sort of nature I think you have. I sure hope I'm not wrong because if I am, you're gonna get hurt.'

The driver took a careful gander at Dayle. He assessed the breadth of his shoulders, his total poundage, the hard and fixed expression on his pan.

After he'd done that he said: 'No, you ain't wrong, mister. Me — I like helpin' folks along, and I don't expect nothin' for it. Not a cent. Tell the dame to come on in.'

11

It was good to be on the move again. To sit in a roadster and watch the highway being sucked under your fast-turning wheels, and to know that with every minute you were just that much nearer the border. Spoff sure was making that car move some. He'd been in the driving seat for seven hours without a break and for most of that time the speed needle had flickered between sixty and eighty. He showed no sign of getting tired either. Yeah, maybe Spoff was no good elsewhere, but he was okay behind a steering wheel. As he glanced at him, Duke looked almost like he was grateful.

Right now it was breaking daylight, and to their right the tip of the sun was emerging over the horizon. Ahead the road was straight, grey and empty; Duke ceased thinking about Spoff. He started to think about something else. Something a whole lot more important. He started to think about himself, and about the empty condition of his belly.

He twisted round and looked at Al. Al was sprawled across the back seat, but it wasn't so easy to see him. Some of those dresses were still hung up there, and they concealed all of Al except the lower half of his legs. Duke put out a hand and parted the materials. Al looked like he'd been sleeping.

Duke said to him: 'We're making nice going. But you know what — I'm hungry. I'm thinking maybe we ought to pull in some place and take ham and eggs.'

The idea seemed to make a big impression on Al. He sat up and nodded. 'Sure. We can't go on like this without a break. Anyway, we've gotta eat.'

Spoff had been listening. Without taking his gaze of the road he told them: 'We've gotta stop soon for gasoline. If we don't, we're gonna stop without it. I figure we can have a tightner at the same time.'

'Yeah,' Duke said. 'But get this — we ain't hangin' about for long. I figure we're okay for the rest of today at least, but we ain't takin' chances.'

They were silent for a time. Then Al asked: 'What'yer figure Lucy'll do?'

Duke didn't have many doubts about that. 'She'll go on runnin' till she can't run any more. Then she'll be lost. Right now I guess she'll be wanderin' around some place trying to find just where she is. And she'll be too scared to ask anyone, which suits us. She'll be picked up, but not for a while.'

Al asked: 'You don't think she might go right back to that cop?'

'She might if she could find him, but I figure she'll have run too far away for her to do that. She was certainly covering the ground mighty fast when last we saw her. Lucy was so scared she couldn't do anything but run. No — she's cut our time down by a day or two, maybe, but not enough to make any real difference.'

That seemed to satisfy Al. The sun was starting to get warm when they sighted a road café. It wasn't much better than a wood hut, but it had a gasoline pump outside and a big notice that said EATS. Spoff eased his foot off the gas pedal and pressed it on the brake. They were stopping in front of the joint when they saw something that made Spoff whip his foot back again to the accelerator.

It was a highway patrol cop on a motorcycle. He was drawing away from the café and was only twenty yards ahead of them. Duke gave out a hard curse and dragged on the handbrake. As the motor stalled he bawled at Spoff: 'What's got into you? Ain't you seen a cop before?'

There was sweat on Spoff's pan when he croaked: 'He could be lookin' for us.'

'So what? Right now, he hasn't seen us. He got his back to us, and he's movin' away. But you wanta overtake him so he can get a long gander? Take a hold on yourself. He ain't wantin' us, but if he had been, you wouldn't have helped us any.'

They climbed out of the car.

A man who had an apron round his fat middle and looked like he could use a shave, was standing in the doorway. He said: 'Hiyer,' and asked if they wanted to eat.

'We ain't here on a social call,' Duke

114

told him. 'Get us ham and eggs three times with plenty of coffee — and get the tank filled with gasoline.'

The café owner yawned. 'Don't often get custom as early as this,' he said. 'I guess I wouldn't have been up at all if that cop hadn't called, but I had to fix him with some coffee. I guess it pays to side right with the law.'

He eased inside. They followed and sat themselves at a dirty glass-topped table. The café owner went behind the counter. He pulled out a big pan and put it over an oil stove. Inside a minute the place was filled with the aroma of frying. Then he went outside and filled the car tank. When he came back the meal was ready. When he'd served them the boys ate fast.

'Say you sure look like you enjoy yer food,' the café owner said. 'Or maybe yer haven't eaten for a long time.'

None of them answered. They were too hungry for conversation. But he wasn't discouraged.

'I guess when yer in the sellin' line you have big distances to travel, and yer get mighty hungry that way.'

Spoff had nearly finished. He looked up and asked: 'What makes you think we're sellin' anything?'

'Hell — that ain't so hard to figure out. Not when you've got the car half-filled with dresses . . . '

Suddenly his voice seemed to die away. He looked vacantly at them and then through the open door towards the car. All the colour had gone out of his unshaven pan. The muscles round his mouth started to do a rapid twitch as if he was having an invisible massage. Duke, who noticed, had a cup of coffee in his hand. He was going to suck some of the liquid in, but he didn't get that far. Instead he asked: 'What's on your mind, bud?'

The man with the apron didn't seem to hear at first. Then he shook his head violently.

'Nothin' — nothin' at all. I — I've just remembered I forgot to order my provisions for the week — yeah, that's it. Forgot all about it. I'll have to phone town right now or I'll have nothin' to sell — ' He went into a room at the far end of the counter. He moved quickly, and he shut the door behind him.

The boys stopped eating and drinking. They stayed dead still, just looking at each other.

Then Al said: 'You know somethin' — I don't like this. I don't like the way that punk's behaving.'

Duke nodded. 'Me neither. I think maybe we'll listen to this phone talk.'

They got up quietly and moved towards the closed door. Duke turned the handle. The door didn't move. It had been locked from the inside. He pressed his ear against the wood. The café owner's voice came to him. Low but distinct. Al and Spoff were listening too.

The voice said: 'I want police headquarters, operator, and make it fast!'

Al didn't hesitate. He had his gun out before the sentence was finished. He put a slug into the keyhole. For a second the place was filled with the row of the explosion and the screeching of torn metal. Then he threw himself at the door. It didn't move.

Duke grabbed Al's gun arm. 'It's fixed

with a bolt,' he breathed hoarsely. 'That bolt's on the inside, and we can't see just where it is. You may have to plug the whole door, and we ain't got that much time — '

Al tried to force his arm. 'Are you crazy? We can't let him get on to the cops!'

'Pipe down! He's done that already. If we stop him right now it won't make any difference. The operator's had the call, and it can be traced back here. We gotta get out and do it fast.'

Al hesitated. His finger twitched round the gun trigger.

But not for long. He knew that what Duke had said was right. They had to get out. Somehow, in some way, the alarm was being spread. Their descriptions were being circulated. Al pushed the gun into his pocket and they ran towards the car.

When they were again hitting the road Spoff said. 'What's happened, Duke? It ain't more than a few hours since we left the shack. How can a dragnet have got out in that time?'

Duke didn't answer, he was breathing

hard. Then he said: 'I guess it's Lucy. I was wrong. She musta gone back to that flatfoot. I'm gonna fix Lucy — '

They had covered a couple of miles when they saw a secondary highway. On Duke's orders, Spoff stopped while a map was checked. 'This can do us,' Duke announced. 'It keeps bearing south, and that's the way we wanta go. And I figure it'll be safer than the main road — until we find some place to lay up.'

Al leaned forward from the back seat. He gripped Duke's shoulder. 'What'yer mean, lay up? We can't afford to rest any place. We've done plenty of that. We've gotta keep movin' for that border.'

Duke swore. It was just a single word, and he said it softly. An oath on velvet. 'We won't be able to move for long. Every highway'll be blocked before the day's much older. That means every car'll be checked. I tell you, we've got to find some quiet place where we can cover up and work out the next move.'

Spoff turned the roadster on to the narrower surface. Then he gave out a whine. 'Yeah — but where are we gonna find a quiet place? We don't know this part of the country.'

Duke bunched his fists and thrust them deep in his jacket pockets. 'Relax,' he told him. 'Just keep driving . . . I'll tell you when to stop.'

Neither Spoff nor Al liked that. They didn't appreciate having to rely on Duke's intuition. They would have liked to have been given more details. But Duke wasn't in the sort of mood for more questions.

Spoff couldn't press along so fast now. The road wasn't straight, and there were some unexpected turnings. But occasionally they saw houses. Nice-looking houses in their own grounds. This looked as though it could be a top-grade residential area for the town of Barras Hills.

Duke started to take a lot of interest in those houses. He sat up and peered closely at them. It was when they approached one that was smaller than the others, but set well back from the road, that he said: 'Go up the drive. We're makin' a call here.'

Spoff looked uncertain. But he turned

120

in at the open gate and rolled up the drive.

The place was built of white stippled stone and there was a veranda running the length of the first floor. A grey De Soto convertible was parked outside the front door.

As they got out Duke said: 'We're gonna act polite — at first. I wanta case this joint so we have to have a reason for calling. Right now Spoff's the reason. I'm gonna say Spoff's been taken sick and do they mind if he rests awhile.'

Spoff looked surprised now. He gave Duke a baffled glance.

'Say, I don't feel sick or nothin'. What do I do?'

'Just act your natural self. Anyone who hasn't seen you before would think you'd got somethin' real bad.'

Al wasn't too comfortable either. 'Say — I'd like to know more about what's on your mind. I don't go for just walking into a house. It might be filled with a whole heap of folks we can't handle.'

'Then we'll ease out — when Spoff's feeling better. And they won't think a thing.'

With Duke well in the lead they mounted the four stone steps to the open front door. Duke pulled on an old-fashioned iron bell-ring. They heard it clanging somewhere in the back. Al and Spoff shuffled nervously.

A little fat man, who blinked through rimless glasses merged out of the shadows in the hall. He was wearing a long white linen coat that was flecked with what looked like dabs of oil paint. He regarded his visitors as though he wasn't so sure about them, and he smoothed down his curly grey hair as he spoke.

'Hello — what can I do for you?' It was the quiet uncertain voice of a man who is used to being kicked around. Duke gave him a broad grin.

'I'm sorry to interrupt you. You see, we've been motoring through the night, and our friend here — the little guy — started to feel ill. His heart, I guess. He keeps having attacks. So we thought maybe you wouldn't mind giving him a chair so he can rest a while.'

He looked at Spoff.

'Yeah,' he said, 'your friend sure

122

doesn't look so good. I guess Edie won't mind him coming in. Edie's my wife — '

He stood aside, and they entered the hall. He led the way into the morning room. It was nicely furnished, and the open french windows gave out on to an ornamental garden. Al helped Spoff into a deep chair.

'Take it easy,' Duke told him. 'You'll soon be feelin' okay now you've got some place cool to rest.'

Spoff had a glazed expression. He needed time to get acquainted with this kind of treatment from Duke. He made a noise at the back of his throat. The man in the white coat blinked at him with real sympathy.

'Edie'll know what to do. I'll go get her.'

Duke looked around. Then he asked: 'Your wife must be some woman to run a swell little place like this — or does she have help?'

'No. Edie does all the work around here. I have my studio at the top. You see, I'm an artist. I paint portraits.'

Duke said that was swell. The artist went out. They heard him talking to Edie in the back, but couldn't make out what he was saying. A couple of minutes later he returned with his wife.

It was then that the boys understood why this man looked like he was used to being kicked around. If Edie had been born to wear pants instead of skirts she'd have made a ball player or maybe a heavyweight fighter. She was three inches taller than her husband, and all of her poundage looked like it was hard muscle. But her pan made the biggest impression. It was sallow, oval, and a massive nose seemed as though it had been rivetted on to the centre. She had the sort of brown eyes that are always hot with fury. Mostly fury against her husband. Her jet black hair was pulled back tight.

She looked carefully at all three in the way a rancher does when he's putting a price on low-grade cattle. Her voice was loud, and it rasped: 'Tom tells me one of you has had a heart attack, but none of you look so good to me.'

Spoff shut his eyes and lay back. It was a good and realistic move, but he only did it because he didn't want to have to look at this woman. Duke and Al ran their hands across their chins.

'We've been driving hard for three days, lady,' Duke told her. 'No time to stop much because we're on urgent business. I guess that's why our buddie here folded up. We'd be mighty grateful if he could rest.'

'Sure he can rest, and maybe I'd better phone for the doctor.'

'That ain't necessary. This sort of thing happens often. He'll be okay soon.'

Edie turned on Tom. 'Go fix some coffee,' she ordered crisply, 'while I ring for the doc. I still figure he needs proper attention,'

Duke, who had been sitting on the arm of a chair, got up and eased slowly towards Edie. That broad smile was on his pan. 'I said he don't need a doctor, and I ain't aimin' to trouble you.'

Her brown blobs narrowed on each side of her nose. 'It won't be any trouble. And while a man's sick in my home he's going to have the proper treatment. Maybe he ought to go to hospital.'

Duke was only a few inches from the

woman, He wasn't as tall as she, but that didn't seem to be troubling him any. And the smile on his pan started to fade. He called toward Tom, who was on his way out to the kitchen.

'Hey, you! Come right back. You can make the coffee when I tell you.'

For a second Edie went blank. Then her eyes became so narrow they could hardly be seen. And she compressed her lips so they hardly moved when she spoke. She was the kind of woman who looked on her husband as her own exclusive punchbag. She could swipe him as hard as she liked, but no one else could take a poke.

'Say — don't you dare talk to Tom that way. You ain't running this residence. You can get right out now if you feel that way.'

Tom stood on his left foot, rubbing the ankle with the toe of his right shoe. Duke said to him: 'Are you expectin' any visitors today?'

The question came out fast. So fast that Tom answered without thinking. 'No — we don't have many friends around these parts.'

Duke said: 'I ain't surprised when the place is run by an outsized no-good like this dame.'

Edie went white. It seemed like the foundations of her empire were being threatened. She braced herself and aimed the flat of her hand at Duke's cheek

That move didn't do her any good. And it didn't do Duke any harm. He caught her hand while it was still moving. He gave it a hard twist, at the same time pushing sideways, Edie gave out a sharp yelp and ended on the carpet. She hit it with a bump that shook the room.

Tom looked like a man who was in the middle of a bad dream. He'd never seen this sort of thing happen to Edie before. He still wasn't convinced that it could happen to her. Maybe there was a mistake somewhere. Maybe he hadn't seen it right. No man was tough enough to push Edie around!

But a big change had come over Edie. Maybe for the first time in her life she was scared. Suddenly she realised that these folks didn't look like ordinary travellers. The one who was supposed to be sick — he was standing up now and leering at her. The tall one was lighting a cigarette from Tom's silver box and looking as though he saw women slapped down every day. And the one who'd done the slapping — he had a gun in his hand.

It took Edie quite some time to get hold of the fact that a gun was aimed at her. She'd never seen a firearm before. Edie wasn't used to this kind of pitch. She became hypnotised by the black void inside the barrel. Death could come out of there. Death at the flip of a finger. She crawled on to her knees and glanced towards Tom. He was no help. Tom's jaw was unhinged, and he was breathing like a fish through gills.

Duke said to her: 'Get up, sister, then sit yourself down. The same goes for that punk painter of yours. I wanta talk to you two.'

Edie got up. She was like a semi-deflated blimp balloon as she staggered towards the chair Spoff had been using. Tom was no better. He subsided on a settee and looked glad for the rest.

Duke nodded at them. He told them

they were doing better. Then he said to Spoff: 'Go run the car into their garage.'

Spoff went out fast. He was glad Duke had reminded him of the car. They didn't want that to be seen. It would easily be recognised.

Still aiming the gun at the couple, Duke glanced at Al. 'Rustle up something to drink. Get out a bottle of whisky.'

Edie showed a flicker of fight. Just a flicker. No more. And it soon died. 'We don't keep hard liquor in this house. I don't approve of it and — '

She faded out as Duke took a half step in her direction, 'That's a pity, sister, but I guess we can soon put that right. We're gonna be staying with you for a few days and we like to be entertained the nice way. A case of bourbon is gonna be one of the things you'll buy for your guests.'

Tom was clutching the lapel of his white coat. It was stained by grease from his fingers. He swallowed twice and asked: 'What is this? Are you stick up men?'

Duke laughed and so did Al. But there was not much humour in their efforts.

'Stick up men! Geeze no! Right now we're guests and you're gonna look after us good. Get it? And you're not gonna mention to anyone that we're here. You see, we're kinda famous and we don't want too much publicity.'

Edie and Tom took in the information. Tom was the first to react. 'Say — you must be criminals on the run!'

Al said: 'This guy's smart. The way he pulls in the clues he oughta be a cop.'

But Tom didn't seem to be listening. He had something more to say. 'You can't keep us prisoners in our own home. We've both got to get out sometime or folks'll wonder where we are.'

'That's right,' Duke said. 'And we're not gonna stop you goin' out — provided one of you always stays right here to keep us company. That way we can be sure you won't do anything stupid and spoil our rest, because if the cops should come along, then the one who's with us would collect a slug before the law could do a thing. Yer understand?'

Edie croaked up. 'You mean you'll always keep one of us here as — as a hostage?'

'Nicely put, lady. I go for good English. That's just how it is, so it's gonna be better to keep quiet if you wanta preserve this love nest.'

There was a long silence. Tom went on fingering the lapel of his coat, and Edie gazed blankly at nothing. It was Tom who broke it. He said: 'What — what have you done?'

'That sure is an interesting question,' Duke answered smoothly. He glanced at a clock on the desk in the corner. 'Say, it's around time for the news flashes on the radio. Maybe the announcer'll tell you.'

There was a midget radio beside the clock. Al turned it on. The news flashes were coming through. Right now, the announcer was giving on some political crisis in Europe. Then he read out a ball game result. It was after that that all became interested.

The news reader said: 'Three men who took part last Wednesday in a raid on an armoured pay truck, which was on its way from Chester City to the local oil fields, are now believed to be in Barris Hills area. They were recognised this morning at a highway café by the owner. They may be trying to reach the southern border. These men are armed and are dangerous. All roads are being watched. State police department ask — '

Al switched off at a signal from Duke, who looked again at Edie and Tom. Their appearance was getting less healthy.

'Maybe that helps you,' Al suggested. 'I'm gonna be frank with you. Right now we're in a spot. We need time to lie up and figure things out. That's why we're here. I guess no one'll think of looking in the home of a nice respectable artist.'

'That's right,' Al said. 'And maybe while we're here he'll paint our portraits.'

They both laughed again and some colour rushed back into Tom's face. Spoff came in. He took a cigarette from the box and lighted it.

'The car's tucked away,' he said. 'But there's only room for one in that garage.'

Duke asked Tom, 'Is that your De Soto outside?'

When Tom nodded, Duke said: 'Well it won't have any shelter while we're here. We're kinda particular about our auto. We like to keep it out of the wind, so it'll stay inside your garage.' He thought for a moment before adding, 'Were you goin' any place?'

'I was going into town to collect some paints. It's a special delivery and they phoned me just before you came to say they'd arrived — but it doesn't matter. I don't feel like work now.'

Duke said, 'You're goin' into town to get those paints just like nothing's happened, see? And remember, if anything goes wrong, it's gonna be just too bad for Edie, because Edie'll be right here with us.'

Tom said in a flat kind of way that he understood. Then Al thought of something. Something that made him talk loud and fast.

'Say, if this bum paints portraits, then folks are bound to come here so as to pose for him. Ain't that right?'

Duke slowly pursed his lips. He let out a long and slow whistle. They were all looking at Tom. Duke's tones were like crushed silk when he said: 'So you weren't on the level when you said you didn't have visitors.'

'I'd forgotten about that — really I had.'

Duke said: 'I ain't so sure, but it don't matter much. Is anyone due today?'

Tom said some folks were.

'It's a double portrait I've been commissioned to do. A newly wed couple, name of Van Howlan. It's an important job because their families have a whole lot of influence around these parts. They are due at three for the first sitting.'

Duke nodded.

'That'll be okay,' he said. 'You have them up in your studio like nothing's happened. You paint their mugs and make them look swell. We'll keep right out of your way. We wouldn't think of lettin' you down. But Edie'll be right with us, won't you Edie? And it'll be too bad for both of you if you start tryin' to slip any messages. The cops may come if you do that, but you two won't live to see them through the door.'

The sweat was oozing out of Tom's brow. It had also damped his grey hair. He was in bad shape. 'Maybe I'd better put off the appointment. I — I don't much feel like it today.'

Duke strode towards him. He got hold of the greasy coat lapels and jerked the artist to his feet. Then he shifted a hand to his collar and twisted it so that his breath came in hard gasps.

'You'll work as usual and you'll like it. You and that dame of yours are gonna behave as normal, see? Nobody's gonna have any reason to think there's a thing wrong. Remember, you play this the smart way and you won't get hurt. But if you ain't smart you'll both be cold meat. Now — let's get organised. When were you goin' into town to collect those paints?'

Tom was going that morning. That was why he'd got out the De Soto.

'Okay,' Duke told him, 'you can get started, I ain't the sorta guy who'd interfere with artistic inspiration.'

He turned to Edie. She flinched away from him. Edie had been tamed.

'And you — go get us something to eat. And fix it quick. We don't like to be kept waiting. Spoff'll go with you.'

When they were alone Duke gave the boys a satisfied smile.

'We're okay for a few days,' he told them. 'Things have worked out nice. Now we're gonna be able to do some real planning.'

12

There was no airport at Barras Hills. The town wasn't big enough for that. But a mile out of the place there was a big cleared space where planes could land and take off. It was here that a Dakota came in just before midday. It was a private charter plane but it wasn't carrying much of a payload. Just a man and a young woman. The rest of the seats were empty, and since it had been hired by the State police department that might be taken as a waste of taxpayers' money. Maybe it was. But this too was urgent and way back in Parry Falls a Dakota had been the only plane immediately available. When they stepped out of the machine Dayle said to Lucy: 'We're going to headquarters — and the car's right here for us.'

A police car cruised along the field and they got inside. A man wearing a panama and smoking an acrid cigar put out his hand when they were settled in the back.

'I'm Tewle,' he told them. 'Captain Tewle and I run the department in these parts. It sure was a surprise to get that call saying you were flying out here. I'm not sure you ain't wasting your time, though. That mob ain't been picked up yet, so I guess they musta got clear of this area.'

Dayle looked disappointed. 'I thought we'd have got some line on them by now,' he said. 'I can't see them getting far with every road blocked. That's why I decided to come right here when I got the flash about them being in the highway café, This is the nearest town to that place and the chances are they'd have to come through it some way.'

Tewle shrugged a pair of heavy shoulders. 'They ain't been in Barras Falls. If they had they'd have been seen okay. My boys are smart and I have plenty of them.'

He looked hard at Lucy. She was sitting between them and she didn't look like she was exactly relaxed. Lucy still hadn't got used to being on social terms with cops.

'Say,' Tewle asked, 'who are you? An operator?'

Dayle answered for her. 'You can call her Lucy. She used to work in with that mob, but that isn't so now. She's being wise and she's helping me. She knows plenty about them, and what they're likely to do, so she could be useful. Lucy's under open arrest, but right now there's only you and me need to know that.'

Tewle opened his eyes wide. He looked interested. 'That's a big move to tote her around. Have you had an okay to do it?'

'Yeah. Headquarters didn't much like it, but they've given me a free hand on this job so they couldn't refuse.'

By now they were entering the centre of Barras Hills. The traffic was moving slowly and there was plenty of reason for that. Every fifty yards it was being halted while officers made a check of the passengers. It was thorough work and Dayle liked to see it. He said so and Tewle looked pleased.

'I told you they won't slip past my boys,' he said.

139

As the car stopped outside police headquarters Lucy flicked dust off the new dress that had been bought for her. Then she said: 'I sure am glad I'm not with Duke now. But you know what — knowin' Duke, I figure the last thing that punk'll do will be to try to come through this town.'

They were sitting in Tewle's office before Dayle answered Lucy. He said, 'I've been thinking along the same lines as you. But just what do you think he'll do?'

Lucy smoothed her lip paint with the end of a finger. She'd slapped on plenty of make-up but it didn't hide her bruises. She said; 'He might try to hide out some place near that café. He's too smart to try to break through a cordon.'

Tewle pulled hard on his cigar. His face temporarily disappeared behind a cloud of smoke. 'There ain't any place for that mob to hide out in these parts,' he said, and he spoke like he was sure of his facts. 'We don't have deserted farms. This is prosperous country.'

Dayle gave Lucy a grin. 'It looks as if we could be wrong there kid,' he said.

At around this time the artist was buying his paints. In the shop the tubes were put out before him, but Tom wasn't concentrating. In fact, he hardly looked at them before telling the assistant that they were okay and parcel them up.

Next he went to a liquor store. He was glad he'd remembered that because just before he'd driven away that big hoodlum called Al had shouted after him to be sure and bring back some bourbon. He bought two bottles. And on the way out of the store he almost walked into patrol officer Deegan.

Deegan was one of the few people he knew well. Edie didn't approve of him having a lot of friends. But she didn't worry much about Deegan because this cop was a kind of artist himself. He painted landscapes as a recreation, and Tom sometimes helped him with his work. Deegan pushed his cap back as he saw Tom.

'Say, what's happening to you? Been buying hard drink? This sure is something. I thought you didn't touch the stuff.'

Tom felt uneasy. He looked uneasy, too. 'It's — it's a tonic,' he said weakly. 'I haven't been feeling so good and — '

Deegan slapped his back. 'Sure, I know. But be careful how you get that stuff in the house. You don't want your wife to see.'

Officer Deegan continued his patrol with a wide grin spread over his pan. Tom decided he wanted a drink — a soft drink at the drug store. There he'd be able to think. To try to sort things out.

He bought himself a banana split, sat down at a quiet corner table and wondered what he ought to do. He'd never come across mobsters before. Of course he knew something about them. He'd seen them on the movies, and read about them in books, and he figured he had a pretty good idea of how they went about their work

And he had no doubt that those hoodlums who'd moved into his house were as tough as any in the States. They must be to raid an armoured car. And when they said they'd kill Edie if he did anything right now, they meant just that.

There could be no arguing about that. They were desperate and they could be butchers.

Tom shivered in spite of the heat. He could see what would happen if he went squealing to the cops. They'd raid the place. There'd be a gunfight. Yeah — in the end the cops would break in all right. But Edie would be found with a bullet in — He shivered again.

'But you've got to do something — got to do something,' he told himself. The subconscious order kept repeating itself like a trip hammer in his brain.

But what could he do? They were trapped. Both of them were trapped. Why were they trapped? Because they were defenceless. They were unarmed. Yeah, that was it. They were unarmed.

Suppose he got a gun?

Maybe that was the answer. With a gun he could wait his time then hold them all up while Edie phoned for the cops. It could be easy. They'd never expect it of him.

But he didn't know how to use a gun. And in this state you couldn't buy one without going first to the police for a permit.

Yet the permit was only a formality. Just a way of letting the police know who had firearms and booking down the serial numbers. They had no power to refuse anyone unless he was a convicted criminal. And having got the permit the man at the gun shop would be able to show him how to use it.

The banana split was untasted. Tom's artistic brain was reeling at the prospect. At the boldness of his own imagination. He wondered if he'd have the guts. If he had the nerve to go through with it. He wasn't sure because he wasn't any hero. In fact he was just yellow. If he hadn't been yellow he'd have done something when they were pushing Edie around.

Tom picked up his parcels and moved slowly out to the police headquarters.

★ ★ ★

An officer put a long printed form on the desk in front of Captain Tewle.

'It's an application for a gun permit,' he

said. 'From a guy name of Thomas Pile. We've checked the records and he's okay.'

Tewle picked up a pen and glanced at the written-in particulars.

He said to Dayle, 'These days folks are going gun crazy. Get a load of this — here's a guy who paints portraits wants a permit for a revolver. An artist. Gee, whoever heard of one of them guys living the hard way? Still, there's nothing against him, so he'll have to have the permit, I guess. That's the law, and I can't go against it.'

Dayle watched idly while Tewle scrawled his signature at the bottom of the form and handed it back to the officer. Then he returned to his stance in front of the window. That was the way he'd been standing for the last hour. Right in front of the window. Just looking into the street and waiting — waiting — for a report that would send him on his way. For some lead that would guide them to the mob. So far, there'd been nothing. Nothing to work on at all.

Lucy had fallen into a deep sleep in one of the chairs. That girl was played out. And Lucy snored a bit. Not much but enough to tarnish the glamour. Her occasional nasal grunt was all that broke the heavy stillness in the office. A stillness of tension and depression.

Although there was another sound. But it was so faint that neither Dayle nor Tewle really noticed it. It was the muffled sound of voices. It could be an argument, but it was taking place at the other side of the door and at the far end of the corridor, so it didn't matter much. It only started to matter when Patrol Officer Deegan pushed into the office.

Deegan was in so much of a hurry that he forgot to salute Tewle. His words came out in breathless chunks.

'I'm sorry, sir,' Deegan said. 'But I figure this is important. I know this guy who has just got a gun permit and it seems to me like there's something wrong somewhere. He ain't the type who'd want a gun — not unless he was plenty scared. He paints folks, he doesn't plug them. I met him a couple of minutes ago right here in the headquarters. He was folding the permit away but I caught sight of it. I've tried to persuade him to tell me what's wrong, but he won't say a thing.'

Deegan wiped sweat away from the band of his cap. He replaced it lightly on his head before resuming. 'And that ain't all, sir. Not a half hour ago I met him coming out of a liquor store. Maybe that don't sound so bad, and it wouldn't be for you or me. But he doesn't drink. He never tastes a drop. His wife won't have it in the house. What with him buying liquor then a gun, I'm wondering just what's happening.'

Tewle wasn't impressed. He told Deegan so. 'Listen,' Tewle said harshly, 'you're getting too smart, and that's worse than being too dumb in this business. This guy's entitled to a gun permit. He's got it. He's entitled to buy liquor. He's bought it. So what in tarnation am I expected to do? Do you want me to feed him the liquor in a drip bottle and show him how to load the gun?'

Officer Deegan didn't give up easy. He mopped his pan and started again. 'But I tell you I know this guy and that's what makes it look all wrong. He's a nice guy.

He's a good artist. I know, because I paint myself. He ain't the sort to have enemies, so I don't see why he should want a gun. And a smell of the cork would put him out, so I don't see why he should suddenly take to drink. Particularly when his wife bans it — and if you'd met his wife you'd know what I mean. I tell you, there's something screwy and I figure we oughta find out what it is.'

Tewle was beginning to be impressed. There was an urgency about Deegan that you just couldn't ignore. And Deegan was a good, reliable officer, too. Not the sort to hot himself with crazy ideas.

Dayle moved from the window and stood by the desk. At first he'd only half listened to Deegan, but his interest had quickly increased. Tewle examined the glowing tip of his cigar. Then he said: 'Okay, Deegan, you win. I'll talk to this artist. Send him in.'

Deegan looked uncomfortable. Like a kid who has been yelling for candy and finds he doesn't like it when he gets it. 'I can't do that right now, sir. He wouldn't stay in the building and I'd no power to hold him. But I know where he'll be. He'll be at Jackson's gun shop, fitting himself out with a nice piece of artillery, I'll have him here in just five minutes.'

Tewle nodded. 'Do that,' he said. 'And make it snappy. I've got plenty on my mind today.'

Deegan was easing towards the door when Dayle spoke. Dayle had been thinking fast. Now he acted on a hunch. 'I'll go along with you, Deegan,' he said. 'If this guy refused to stay in the building to please you, I guess he may not be willing to come back to it, and we still can't force him. He ain't under suspicion for anything. It may be necessary to ask him a few questions right there in the gun shop.'

Tewle was looking thoughtful. He said: 'You wouldn't be doing this just to help the routine work of my department. Maybe you're seeing a tie-up with those hoods?'

'There's just a chance and I can't afford to ignore anything,' Dayle told him as he moved out behind Deegan.

Jackson's gun shop was over the road

on a turning off the main street. Behind the grilled windows there was a big display of shooting irons. Everything from elephant rifles to smooth-bore shot guns, from big and cumbersome .45 revolvers to tiny pearl handled Derringer automatics.

Inside the shop Jackson was selling the artist a Derringer. He had slipped out the six-chamber magazine and was showing how the gun was loaded.

'It's the easiest automatic to handle on the market,' Jackson was saying. 'After each shot the empty shells expel themselves and when — '

Dayle eased up and lifted the Derringer gently out of Jackson's hand before the gunsmith knew he was there.

'Maybe you forgot to mention that any gun's worse than useless if the owner's not been properly trained in how to handle it,' he said.

Jackson glared hard at Dayle then at Deegan. He recognised Deegan and made a good guess as to Dayle's occupation. He decided not to act tough, even though they were interfering with a business deal.

'This guy's got a permit and he came

in to buy. I'm selling. That's all I know, and it's all I have to know.'

Dayle gave him a grin. 'That's okay. We ain't worrying any about you.'

The permit was on the counter. Dayle picked it up and read the name *Thomas Pile*. In answer to the printed questions his age had been entered as fifty-two, his previous experience of firearms as nil.

Still holding the Derringer, Dayle put a hand on the artist's elbow and guided him away from the counter and to a chair at the far end of the shop. Tom made no attempt to resist. He sat down almost gratefully. Since he'd been granted the permit he'd become more scared with each passing second and now he was near to total collapse. The earlier fight had gone out of him.

Dayle pulled out a packet of cigarettes and gave one to Tom. He took it with a shaking hand. Then Dayle asked: 'Just what did you want a gun for?' He put the question gently.

'For personal protection — like I said when I made the application.'

Dayle nodded sympathetically. 'Sure.

151

But who do you think you're gonna protect with a gun like this?'

'I — I don't know — it's just that there are so many hoodlums around.'

Dayle slowly examined the magazine of the Derringer. The gunsmith had loaded it with six shells. He slipped it into the butt and cocked the firing pin. Tom watched him in a fascinated way.

'This gun's all ready to shoot with,' he said. 'Now I want you to aim it at me so I can see how you'd shape up if I was a hoodlum — go on, take it.'

Tom blinked with a kind of weak desperation. After a flaming period of hesitation he took the Derringer. He held it as though it was red-hot and he tried to insert two fingers at the same time into the trigger guard. Both of them stuck.

'Now aim at me and try shooting,' Dayle ordered.

'I can't do that,' Tom bleated. 'You're a cop, I guess. I can't shoot at you.'

'That's my risk. I want to see how smart you are with a gun. Shoot, Tom!'

'I won't — not at you.'

'Okay. Then shoot at the floor.'

It was half a minute before he sorted out his trigger finger and got it into place. Then, aiming the barrel down, he fired. There was a brief and not very loud crack. The slug sped along at about two feet above the ground and buried itself in the front of the counter. But it wasn't the slug that caused the most interest. It was the gun itself. That Derringer seemed to jerk itself out of the flaccid grip. Then it became airborne. It flew backwards past Tom's grey head and bounced off the wall behind him. Tom's pan had shaded to nasty grey. He was in bad condition.

Dayle grinned at him and touched his shoulder by way of reassurance. 'See what I mean?' he said. 'Any hoodlum would have that gun off you long before you could use it. And suppose you did have time to use it — do you think you'd do any damage to him on this kinda form? Of course you wouldn't. Right now, you aimed for the floor and you missed. And you couldn't even hold the gun after you'd fired — not even a little Derringer. The kick jerked it out of your hand — How's about coming clean, Tom, and admitting a gun wouldn't do you much good, and it might do you a whole lot of harm?'

Tom nodded. He tried to say something, but he couldn't. His nerves were stretched so tight he couldn't talk immediately. Dayle gave him time to recover. He figured this was almost the point at which he ought to start asking.

He half lifted Tom to his feet and said: 'Maybe you've something you ought to tell us. We'll go over to headquarters and discuss it over a cup of coffee.'

Tom got a hold on his voice. He said he guessed so. As they moved out Dayle turned to the gunsmith.

'The Derringer's on the floor,' he said. 'One shell's been used. I'll call in sometime and pay for that. But the gun's still for sale.'

13

Tom the artist talked. It hadn't been easy to get him to start, but once he was on his way the words came in sobbing torrents. He gave it all. He gave it while huddled in a chair opposite Tewle's desk. An inch of ash had formed on Tewle's cigar when Tom had finished. Dayle had smoked a cigarette so low it was burning his fingers. And Lucy was rubbing her bruised face and figuring that Duke was a heel, but he was still plenty smart.

Then Tewle said slowly: 'I guess we could get in fast if we wait until dark. Too fast, maybe, for them to hurt anybody.'

Tom got up out of his chair. His pan was contorted as he pleaded with Tewle.

'You mustn't do that,' he gasped. 'You mustn't! However quick you were, they'd get us! I know they would. We wouldn't have a chance!'

Tewle wasn't convinced. 'You don't know our methods,' he said. 'Maybe we can be in your house before that mob know a thing.'

Tom raised both his hands in an imploring gesture.

'Maybe you could. But it'd only take them a second to kill Edie and me. And I know they'd do it. They don't care!'

Dayle gave himself a fresh cigarette. His brain had been working in high gear. He asked Tom: 'Did you say you had a guy and his wife coming to your house to be painted this afternoon?'

'Yeah. A young couple by name of Van Howlan. They're mighty important people. A big local family.'

Dayle said: 'That's fine because they're gonna have something to be big about — '

He pushed over Tewle's external telephone.

'Ring up the Van Howlans and tell them you won't be painting them today. Say you've hurt your finger, say anything. But put them off.'

Tom blinked at him. 'I can't do that. Those thugs said I had to carry on as usual. If they don't appear for a sitting the mob might think anything.'

'Never mind what they think. If you want to come outa this alive you've gotta do what I say. Get on that phone.'

He dialled the Van Howlan's number. Tom gave his message to a servant. He looked worried as he put back the receiver. He said he hoped the Van Howlans wouldn't take offence. Neither Dayle nor Tewle bothered to answer him. They had other things on their minds. The Van Howlans could wait.

Then Dayle asked Tom: 'None of that mob intended to be around if the Van Howlans had come along?'

'No, they said they'd keep right out of the way while I painted in my studio. But they'd keep Edie with them.'

Dayle said: 'That's fine, because it means there's less chance of Lucy and me being recognised.'

It was the sort of silence that precedes a clap of thunder. A silence filled with gathering static. Then all three started to talk. But somehow Lucy's voice was the most penetrating, the most insistent. She was standing and plucking at Dayle's coat.

'Whatyer mean, there's less chance of me being recognised? I ain't aimin' to get that close to them for that sorta thing to happen.'

Dayle pushed her away. 'You're gonna do just what I say,' he told her. 'Now listen, this is the pitch. This afternoon Lucy and me are turning up at the house to have our portraits done. We're gonna be Mr. and Mrs. Van Howlan.'

Lucy's eyes were stretched wide. 'Say, you're crazy! They'll know right away who we are!'

'I figure not. They won't be around. There's no reason for them to start taking a gander at us. Not when they have Edie with them as a hostage. But even if they do look, it won't matter because we're gonna change our appearance. You particularly, Lucy. I figure we might be able to fix you with a nice dark wig. And you could wear a pair of sun glasses Some swell clothes, too, maybe. That way I guess you'll pass.'

Lucy showed a brief flicker of interest at the prospect of the clothes. But it was only a flicker. It was quickly replaced by fear. 'I ain't doin' it. I was willing to help, but didn't expect to have to walk right back among the mob as a stoolie!'

Tewle said something to her. Something that wasn't exactly complimentary. It was not the sort of remark a gentleman should make to a lady. But maybe Tewle figured Lucy was no lady. And he knew as much about his own status as anybody.

Lucy was about to slap back at Tewle, but Dayle interrupted. He set about smoothing her over. 'There ain't a lot of risk,' he told her. 'We'll fix ourselves so we won't be recognised.'

'That sounds fine — but how about getting someone else to go along with you — a woman officer? I've had enough action. Right now I want to relax.'

'Anyone else wouldn't be as good, even if we could get someone. You have the inside knowledge. You know what makes that mob tick. That sorta information could be valuable once I'm inside there.'

It was Tewle who clinched the deal. 'I figure we could recommend you for a state pardon if you took on an assignment like this,' he said. 'Instead of going into a penitentiary, you'd be a heroine. Yeah, a real heroine. The newspaper boys'd lap it up big. You'd be asked to write your life story, and you'd be paid nice dough for it. You'll be missing a lot if you pass up this chance, sister.'

A glitter had appeared in Lucy's eyes. She was seeing herself as big time. And on the comfortable side of the law. With plenty of dough. No jail sentence —

'It's a deal,' she said. 'But don't let anything happen to me. I'm still scared when I think of what they'd do — '

Tewle grinned at her. 'You ain't got a thing to worry about.' He nodded towards the door. 'Now leave us for a while, sister. Dayle and me want to talk in private. We've got a lot of little details to fix.'

14

They were sitting round the dining table. Lunch was over. Now Al was getting down to serious work on the bourbon. So were Duke and Spoff, but they didn't like the liquor on the same scale as Al. Already Al had taken half a bottle and he was just warming up. As he poured himself another deep measure he turned a red, inflamed face at Tom and Edie. 'I sure am glad you've relaxed your rules about not having somethin' to drink in the house,' he said. 'It's much more sociable this way, ain't it?'

Tom looked at the tablemats. Edie stared frigidly into space. It had been a bad morning for Edie — particularly after Tom had gone into town. She'd thought maybe she'd be able to slip out of the house while she was supposed to be cooking the meal. But there hadn't been a chance. All the time one or other of the hoodlums had been in the kitchen watching her. And making wisecracks. Not the sort of wisecracks she was used to hearing. It had been a relief when Tom got back with his paints and the drink. Up to now, that bourbon had held their attention.

Spoff contorted his mean little pan into a caricature of a grin. 'And it was a nice meal you cooked, Edie,' he told her. 'I just can't figure why you and Tom didn't eat any of it, Maybe you don't go for your own home cookin'.'

Duke was grinning too as he glanced at his watch. Then he looked at Tom. 'Say, what time did you say those folks were due to be painted?'

Tom flinched at the phrase. He swallowed at nothing, then said: 'They are due for the first sitting at three.'

'Then you'd better be gettin' ready for them. It's almost that time now. We'll stay right here and keep Edie company. And don't forget, Tom — it'll be too bad if you don't make things seem nice and normal.'

Al tossed down his bourbon. He produced a noise like a bad drain. 'That's right,' he said. 'You paint them two good.

162

We wanta be proud of you.'

They laughed as Tom pushed back his chair. Duke leaned across the table and put a hand on his wrist. He said, 'While you were out we took a long gander at your bank book. We persuaded Edie to show us where it was. There's a sweet package of dough in that account. And right now it ain't doin' anyone any good. But we plan to change that. You're goin' into town again tomorrow morning and you're gonna cash a cheque. You're gonna cash it for five thousand bucks — all in small bills. It's gonna be a present from you to us — see?'

Tom spoke as though emerging from a bad dream. 'Five thousand — that's just about all I have.'

'Sure it is. But that won't worry a talented guy like you. In fact, it oughta be an inspiration. It'll give you a reason for some real hard work.'

Tom shrugged his thin shoulders. He said he'd get the money.

There was a ring from the front door.

Duke signalled the boys to be quiet. Then he said, 'This'll be them. And while

163

you're doin' your painting, just think of Edie here with us — '

Tom closed the room door behind him and moved slowly across the hall. His heart was slamming hard against his chest. He felt weak and helpless.

He opened the front door very slowly. Then he peered with a kind of baffled wonder through his glasses

A sultry looking brunette wearing sun glasses and a swell summer dress stood in front of him. The man beside her also wore glasses. But his were the variety that were used to correct bad sight. This guy had a heavy moustache. It would have needed more than a glance to have recognised them as Lucy and Dayle.

Dayle said: 'Good afternoon. We're Mr. and Mrs. Van Howlan.'

Tom played out his part like he'd been told. 'Come right in,' he told them. 'I'm all ready for you in the studio.'

There was a chauffeur driven car in the drive. Dayle asked: 'If the car comes back later will it be okay?'

Tom told him it would. Dayle gave the

driver a signal and he reversed towards the road.

In the room the boys had been listening intently.

Suddenly they all relaxed. Duke said: 'It's okay, Tom's actin' sensible.'

Tom led the way up the staircase. His studio was a converted attic. Most of the roof had been taken out and replaced with glass. It was hot in there. The place stank of paint and chemicals. Tom locked the door. He took off his jacket, put on a white coat. Dayle and Lucy sank on to a settee.

Dayle fingered his moustache. It didn't feel so comfortable. Lucy felt the same way about her dark wig.

It was like carrying an oven on your head.

Tom looked at them in an expectant way.

'Well — that part's gone okay,' he said in a breathless croak.

'I didn't expect it to be hard,' Dayle said. 'Not that part, I've a hunch the really interesting part's gonna be when I walk downstairs and stick those hoods up.

There might be some resistance and then I'll have to shoot. That means we've gotta time this right and work fast, so let's crack the drill again —

'We'll wait here for a half hour. Just long enough to let them settle down. I figure that a couple of them will doze to sleep, leaving one awake to keep an eye on Edie. That'll make it easier for me to break into the room and show them my artillery. While I'm doing that, you, Tom, use the phone in this studio and ring this number — '

He passed a slip of paper with some figures scrawled on it. Tom folded it carefully in his top pocket.

'That number contacts a phone alarm box just four hundred yards along the road from here. Two carloads of officers are waiting there. When they answer you've just got to say '*We've started*'. That'll be enough. That signal'll bring the boys right down here and I'm trusting I'll have these hoods waiting to be collected.

'But there's gonna be an emergency system. We ain't leaving anything to chance if we can help it. That's where

Lucy comes in. Lucy's coming down with me. But she'll go out the front door and run towards the cops, so she'll be able to give them the message if something goes wrong with the phone alarm.' Dayle passed round his packet of cigarettes. They lighted up and tried to relax. But that was difficult. You don't relax so easy when you're contemplating the possibility of not living out the afternoon. Their minds kept dwelling gloomily on the immediate future. There wasn't much in the way of light conversation. They were calm all right. But it wasn't a nice kind of calm.

Dayle looked at his strap watch. He said: 'I'll give it another five minutes, then we go into action.'

And at that moment the phone in the studio rang.

The persistent call of the bell made them all jerk out of their seats. Instinctively, Tom was moving towards the instrument. Before he could reach it the bell stopped. He turned to Dayle.

'There's an extension downstairs,' he

whispered. 'One of the mob must have answered.'

Dayle waved him aside. He picked up the receiver himself. As he put it to his ear the others grouped round close so as to listen. What they heard made their bellies turn to ice.

A woman's voice was at the other end. A cultured and commanding sort of voice.

' — yes, I'm Mrs. Van Howlan,' it was saying.

Dayle whipped his hand over the mouthpiece so that a terrified gasp from Lucy should not be heard.

The voice continued: 'I want to complain to Mr. Pile about having our appointment cancelled at such short notice. It's too bad just to ring up like that and leave a message with one of the servants. Please tell him the contract for the portrait is off. He hasn't kept his side of the deal and my husband and I are no longer interested.'

There was a click and Mrs. Van Howlan had replaced her receiver. Dayle did the same. Then, after only a moment's hesitation he lifted the receiver off again and dialled a number. He listened — No — clearly the line was dead! He knew the reason. The main phone wires had been severed on the ground floor. The mob was acting fast.

Dayle took a swift glance at the door of the studio. The lock that Tom had turned would not last for long. A single bullet would splinter it and it wouldn't hold out for long under a shoulder attack. But the hoods had to be held up for as long as possible. They'd be on their way up now. The only chance was to play for time. Time in which to think out some way of getting a message to the waiting cops.

Dayle grabbed the settee. With Tom's help, he pushed it against the door, jamming the edge of the back under the handle. That was a help, but there was no other heavy furniture to reinforce it.

He glanced up at the glass roof. At almost the same moment he pulled out a gun from his shoulder holster. He turned to Tom and Lucy.

'We'll be okay,' he said. 'I've just remembered — if I put a couple of shots straight up through the glass the boys from headquarters are sure to hear them. They'll figure something's wrong and they'll be right with us. All we've gotta do is to keep the hoods out of here until they arrive.'

Tom's face was ugly with sweat. It was oozing down the side of his nostrils and on to his mouth and chin. His tones grated as he spoke. 'You can't do that! Once they hear the shots that mob'll kill Edie!'

'We've gotta take that chance. If we don't they'll kill the whole lot of us when — '

The door handle turned quickly. The hinges creaked under pressure. Then a voice came through. It was Duke's voice. And it sounded rough. 'Hey you, open up! We wanta have a little talk with you, Tom.'

But Tom wasn't listening. He was watching Dayle. And Dayle was aiming his gun upwards through the roof glass. But he didn't pull the trigger. Tom saw to that. Tom threw himself at Dayle's gun arm.

It wasn't a formidable kind of attack. Tom wasn't built on the lines of a man who can be tough. But it had the element of surprise. And surprise can count for a lot. It was in this case enough to knock Dayle temporarily off balance.

He reeled backwards with Tom frantically clawing at his wrists. And all the time Tom was hissing: 'Don't shoot — if you do, they'll kill Edie — you mustn't shoot — '

This was no time for sentiment. It was no time for old-world courtesy, either. Dayle figured he'd be wrong to worry about slugging a weaker guy like Tom. He pulled back his left hand then drove it forward on to the artist's glistening chin. It was some punch. It seemed to explode against the angle of the jawbone. Tom went down like a broken spring. He was unconscious before he hit the polished wood floor.

Lucy let out a scream. She wasn't screaming because of what had happened to Tom. It was because the lock had been shattered by a bullet from the outside. The door had burst open under a combined attack, pushing the settee along with it. Duke and Al were coming in. Each was holding a gun.

It was the second time inside a minute that Dayle was caught on the wrong foot. At the moment he'd hit Tom his back had been turned to the door. It was still that way when the hoods came in, and weren't slow to size up the situation. There was nothing slow about Duke at times like this. He said: 'You can drop that gun and turn around so I can look at you.'

Dayle let his gun fall, then he faced Duke.

They looked at each other for quite a time. Duke's pan gradually creased as though he was thinking and finding it an effort.

In the end he said, 'I'm not gonna ask you who you are because I don't go for nursery stories. Just the same — there's somethin' kinda familiar about you, mister. Just take them spectacles off! Go on, take them off — '

Dayle figured that if he didn't do it himself Duke would remove them for him. He pulled the glasses with the blank lenses away from his nose.

Then Duke knew. He knew in spite of the crêpe hair moustache. A flow of blood to his pan turned it to a faint shade of purple. He spoke through half closed lips.

'So it's the cop! Dayle was the name on your identity papers. You sure get around Mr. Dayle, but somehow I figure your career's comin' to a full stop right now. I guess the artist musta talked after all. That's gonna be too bad for him and for Edie. I ain't the type to throw out threats that mean nothin' — '

Al had been looking hard at Lucy. At first Lucy had tried to stare right back through her dark glasses. But she couldn't. She turned away while a glacial terror froze through her guts. Al looked carefully at the bruises, which the powder did not hide. At the set of her body. Then at her hair. He spent a long time considering the black hair. It was his sudden forward movement and the snatching away of the wig that inter-rupted Duke.

Lucy didn't look so smart without that wig. Her genuine platinum strands were

173

no longer long and glittering. They had been cut short and were fixed with clips close to her scalp. Al breathed: 'So it's you, babe — you double-crossin' alley cat . . .'

Duke retreated so he could look at both Lucy and Dayle. But right now most of his attention was being given to Lucy. And it wasn't the sort of attention a girl likes from a man. There was that atmosphere of death about Duke. Of death at its worst. Merciless, cruel. And he whispered to her. That was all. A soft and silken whisper. He said: 'You've bought a bullet, Lucy. And it'll come where it lasts longest and hurts most. You know where — unless you act wise and give me the pitch. Then maybe I might think different. Are there more cops around these parts?'

Dayle put in an answer. 'Sure there are. The place is surrounded. You can't get away.'

Duke ignored him. He repeated the question to Lucy. 'Where are the cops, baby?'

Lucy had taken off the sunglasses. She

174

raised her eyes and looked right at Duke. She asked: 'If I tell you and if I help — will you take me along? I guess it's my only chance.'

The shadow of a grin hovered round the corners of Duke's compressed lips. 'Sure, sure. Maybe you've learned it don't pay to two-time me. You can come along with us.'

Lucy said smoothly: 'Okay, I'm gonna trust you. This place ain't surrounded. But there's a couple of cars full of cops waiting at the call box a few hundred yards down the road on the right. Dayle was goin' to stick you boys up while the artist put a phone call through to them.'

'And it might have worked out that way, sister, if the call hadn't come from the Van Howlan dame. I guess we oughta be grateful to Mrs. Van Howlan, but I ain't got much time for gratitude right now. We're gonna beat it from here and we're gonna drive away from where the cops are waitin'.'

Dayle dragged his eyes away from Lucy. He said, 'You're crazy. You'll never get a couple of miles.'

Duke wasn't impressed. He said so. 'That isn't the way I figure it. The cops aren't goin' to start getting' tough with us. Not when we're carrying you and that Edie dame with us. They won't want to lose one good cop and there'll be some raw publicity if they accidentally shoot up a respectable law-abiding woman. No — with that sorta front I guess we've a nice chance of getting out of this area. Then I have new plans to put into operation.'

Lucy was looking at Duke with only half-disguised admiration.

'Gee, you are smart,' she told him. 'With these folks with us the cops won't even know we've gone for a long time. They'll still be waitin' for the call. We can use the artist's De Soto — but say, what about the artist? We can't leave him. He's due to wake up any time.'

'We ain't gonna leave him. He'll come along too. Mr. Dayle's gonna carry him. You can pick him up, Dayle. We're on our way.'

Tom was still unconscious. He'd collected a punch that would have put down most ring heavyweights. Dayle bent down and took him over a shoulder. At Duke's order, he led the way out of the studio and down the stairs. Lucy was right behind him. Duke and Al, their rods ready, brought up the rear.

In the hall, Duke called for Spoff. He came out of the room, his gun aimed at Edie's back. Edie gave out a grunt when she saw Tom and started to run towards him. Duke pushed her away.

'You can relax,' he told her. 'He's okay. Just been slugged, that's all. But we're goin' on a nice motor ride so as to help him recover.'

The De Soto was parked right outside the front door. Dayle was told to lift the artist into a corner of the back seat. He did that. Spoff pocketed his gun and got behind the wheel. Then Duke gave his instructions.

'Dayle — you'll go in the back too, with me and Edie. Al will be in the front, same as Lucy. And don't let anyone try to do anything smart. That means you in particular, Dayle. If you do, the only payoff you'll get will be in lead.'

But it wasn't Dayle who tried to be smart. They were moving toward the open doors of the De Soto when it happened. Lucy suddenly ran down the drive — screaming.

She'd covered ten yards before any of them realised what had happened. Lucy had been making as if to enter the front when she made a sudden swerve, rounded the car bonnet and dashed towards the gates. And at the same time her desperate, panting screams tore into the sky.

Duke was the first to recover. He yelled: 'Get her — get the bitch!'

Al had his gun up. He couldn't miss. Not at that range. Not with Lucy running in a straight line without any sort of cover. Almost before the echo of the heavy cordite charge had died away Lucy was on the ground — full length and face down. She wasn't moving. Not even twitching.

Duke turned on Al. His pan held all the essence of fury.

'You punk,' he yelled at him. 'That was just what I didn't want you to do! The cops might have heard that! Spoff — get the motor started — '

But Spoff was no longer in the driving seat. He'd flung himself out and was standing right in front of Duke. His narrow face was strained and wild. 'I can't,' he said thickly. 'The key ain't there! The artist musta taken it out. It'll be in his pockets somewhere.'

Duke whipped back his free hand. He slapped the open palm across Spoff's cheek.

'Then get the key out of his pockets! He's in the back of the car. What yer waitin' for?'

Under the impact of the blow, Spoff staggered towards Tom's unconscious figure. He groped frantically about his clothing. That took time. Maybe thirty seconds. Then he gabbled: 'It ain't here. He hasn't got his jacket on. Only this white coat. The key must be in his jacket in the studio!'

The flesh of Duke's face was pulsating. 'Then don't worry about the key,' he bawled. 'Tear out the wires behind the dash and join them up.'

As he spoke he was looking at Spoff. So was Al. That was a bad mistake. It was in that moment of distraction that Dayle decided on some action of his own. He was standing in front and slightly to one side of Duke. He straightened his left-hand so it was stiff. It flashed up towards Duke's throat. The edge of it contacted him over the larynx. The bulge there seemed to jump an inch. Duke's gun hand dropped, and as it did so Dayle grabbed the barrel of the weapon and wrenched it from the now weak fingers.

A split second was needed. It was vital. It would take that time to reverse the gun into a shooting position. It was in that period that Al started to move. Al brought up his own gun. He sighted it at Dayle's head. He forgot about Edie. Edie didn't just grab Al from behind. She did a lot better than that. She hurled herself at him.

The whole of her big poundage landed between Al's shoulder blades. They both crashed to the red gravel, and as they did so a second shot exploded from the gun.

But this slug went up into the air at an

acute angle. It hit the glass roof of the studio. The row of the cordite was joined by a clatter of broken and falling glass

Dayle shifted his stance so he had his back to the car. That way he was able to see all three of the hoods. On the drive there was a flurry of clothes, and for a moment Al could not be seen. He was entirely covered by Edie.

It was a bad situation. Dayle couldn't shoot for fear of hitting the woman.

There was a sudden twist and a grunt, and Al was on his knees. He had an arm round Edie's waist, and he was holding her in front of him. He still gripped his gun. It was aimed over Edie's shoulder at a point centre of Dayle's belly.

Al parted his lips. He spoke between great retching intakes of breath.

'You're gonna get it cop — you ain't gonna be smart any more — not while I'm around you ain't — '

Things can happen fast in the human mind. Particularly when it takes a flashback. Dayle's mind did just that.

He was still looking at Al. But Al was not wearing a civilian suit any more. He

181

wasn't kneeling on a gravel drive. They weren't redwood trees that stood behind him.

Al was in army jungle kit. Torn and dirty. He was still kneeling, but on wet jungle moss. The dense foliage behind him was that of the Solomon Islands — and there was a gun in his hand. An army rifle.

Dayle said quietly: 'You can hide behind a woman, Al. But it won't make any difference. I've got a settling with you, and it ain't just for what's happened here. There are two G.I.s out in the Pacific — remember? I figure they'd have liked me to even this out.'

As he spoke he was walking towards him. Smooth, slow steps. They took him to one side of Al, so Edie was no longer in the way. Al tried to force Edie round so she would still shield him. But she struggled and was too heavy.

Dayle whispered: 'You ain't feeling so good, Al. You're shaking. But you don't have to worry any more. I'm gonna put you out of your misery, bud — '

The bullet that killed Al lifted up the

top of his skull as if it was an eggshell.

Dayle glanced at Duke and Spoff. They were standing still, looking in a bewildered way at what was once Al. Dayle told them: 'It's okay, boys. You won't have long to wait either.'

With his free hand he fished a cigarette out of his pocket. And another sound had broken the still of the afternoon. It was the sound of car sirens coming up the drive . . .

* * *

Tewle pushed his phone away. He looked thoughtfully at Dayle.

'I guess there are some things that just don't add up,' he said.

Dayle was slumped back in the chair opposite. A cigarette was drooping out of the corner of his mouth, and his eyes were closed. He was tired.

'Yeah?' he mumbled. 'What's on your mind?'

'It's about Lucy.'

Dayle slowly opened his eyes.

'Go on — what's the news?'

'The hospital says she's gonna live.'

Dayle dragged himself upright in the chair. Suddenly he was interested.

'Geeze — that's what I've been hoping to hear. That girl sure has earned a State pardon. But say — just what is it that doesn't add up?'

There was a deep grin on Tewle's pan. He gave himself a cigar, lighted it.

Then he said: 'She's got plans for going straight now. But that ain't all. She's just told the doctors she wants to take up art. She plans on learnin' how to paint portraits, and she's gonna ask that artist guy to teach her. She says that way she'll learn how to live a quiet life — '

THE END